My Mother's
Persian Stories

Saeid Shammass & Shaunie Shammass

Cover Painting and Illustrations by Saeid Shammass

KIP - Kotarim International Publishing, Ltd.

KIP – Kotarim International Publishing, Ltd.

Graphic Design by: Laura Gryncwajg
Publisher: Moshe Alon

ISBN 978-965-7238-30-1

Israel 2018

In memory of my mother, Zinat

Table of Contents

Preface

This is a collection of stories that my mother told to her many children before bedtime. We usually fell asleep before the story ended and sometimes, she would doze off in the middle of telling a story. After I had my own children, I had the pleasure of sitting with her, and asked her to retell them to me. In keeping with her tradition, I then told them to my own children.

The custom of telling bedtime stories is ancient. Over the ages, they have passed from one generation to another through oral tradition. Each generation has embellished them in new ways by adding or subtracting some of the details. My mother told these stories to her first born children slightly differently than she told them to those like me, who were born later.

These stories were made by wise and loving souls whose names have been forgotten but whose works have remained eternal. Some have elements of ancient Persian mythology, some are mystical, some are humorous, and some are perhaps allusions to actual historical events.

The number of stories that my mother actually told us was much greater than appears in this book. However, the ones included in this book, as far as I know, are less familiar. In the oral tradition of storytelling, and in the memory of my mother, I have added stories of my own, which are the last three tales in this collection.

My wife, whose mother tongue is English, suggested writing a bilingual book in English and Persian. We wrote the stories together in a way that captures both western and eastern storytelling, while keeping the original flavor of Persian folk tales. We sat for many hours, and discussed many nuances at length until we reached this final version.

I have illustrated the stories using a mixed media approach, combining pictures and drawings. Many images are those that I imagined while listening to the stories as a child.

We wish to thank my sister, Forough Shammass, for her careful reading of the Persian text and insightful comments. We are also grateful to Diane Yerushalmi and Susan Susser for editing the English text and providing many helpful suggestions.

Our greatest wish is that parents everywhere continue the oral tradition of storytelling and retell them to their own children, perhaps embellishing and changing them as they see fit, or even adding new tales of their own.

1

The Bird of Seven Colors

Once upon a day and once upon a time, under the purple dome of the sky, there was a king who had a beautiful bird that could change to seven beautiful colors, sing seven wonderful songs, and dance seven different dances. This extraordinary bird was free to fly from one tree to the other in the king's orchard, but never flew away from the castle because of the king's love. In return, the bird always made the king very happy by singing and dancing.

Many years passed, and the king became older. Whenever he was tired or upset, he came to visit his prized bird. He looked at its seven beautiful colors, and listened to its seven lovely songs, and watched its seven enticing dances, and always became happy again.

One day, the bird stopped singing and dancing. It began eating less and less. Worst of all, the bird's feathers lost all of their beautiful colors and turned a gloomy grey. The king asked his courtiers to find the best doctors to come and cure the bird. Many doctors came and went, but nobody could help the poor creature. So the king asked for the wisest of the wise to come to the palace and give him advice.

Of all the wise men, there was only one with such wisdom and experience. He was an old, old man from a small village far away from the palace. The courtiers sent a carriage to immediately bring him to the castle and examine the bird. The wise man told the king, "This bird is lonely and needs a spouse. You must find another bird of seven colors and bring it back to the palace. As soon as your dear bird sees its companion, its feathers will again change to seven beautiful colors, and sing seven songs, and dance seven dances."

The king, who had many sons, had a bright idea. He summoned all of his sons together and said, "My beautiful bird of seven colors needs a partner. Whoever brings back a worthy mate with feathers of seven colors will be anointed as the next king. Such a journey is perhaps full of adventure and danger, but the one that can find the beautiful bird is worthy of ruling this land."

The king's servants gave each son a horse, an urn full of gold coins, and provisions. But to the youngest prince, who was the king's favorite, they brought no horse, no urn full of coins, and no provisions. The young prince became very upset and complained to his father that he also wanted be given a chance to find the bird of seven colors. "I know how much you love your bird, dear father, and I want you to be happy again," said the favorite son. The king replied, "My dear prince, you are too young to begin such a treacherous quest. It is too dangerous for you to go to unknown places in search of a bird of seven colors. Stay here with me and I will give you all the riches you need to lead a comfortable life." But the young son insisted, and did not stop badgering the old king until he reluctantly agreed to also give his youngest son a horse, an urn full of gold coins, and provisions for the quest.

The princes started out on their journey. The palace gates opened and they rode out of the palace walls with much fanfare. None of them had any idea of how to search for a bird of seven colors. They started to ask people along the way, "Have you ever heard of a seven-colored bird that can also sing and dance? Where is its nest?" But no one had heard of such a thing.

Outside the palace there was a long highway, which was known to lead to different parts of the world. At one point, the highway split in two – one to the west and one to the east. The princes reached this fork in the road and had to choose which way to go. They asked the locals which way was best, and they replied, "The road to the west is known to be free of danger and safe, and everybody travels there. However, the road to the east is full of challenges, and rarely a traveler goes that way."

All of the elder princes chose the safe way to the west. After travelling a while, each one of them came to an interesting city. One prince found himself in a city teeming with markets that sold exotic goods of every kind. Another found himself in a city that had the tastiest food in the world. And others found themselves in cities where there were countless ways to spend money and enjoy life.

When the youngest prince reached the fork in the road, he heard the local people's advice, and thought to himself, "In order to find such a rare and unique bird, it is best to choose the difficult and dangerous path." So, unlike all of his brothers, he rode his horse towards the east.

The young prince travelled a long distance, over many hills and through high treacherous mountains. Many nights he slept on cold bare rocks. He chose his path carefully until finally, he came to a big jungle full of green tangled brush and exotic trees. He found a hidden path that meandered through the jungle and thought that, perhaps, the bird of seven colors could be found there.

At night, he carefully chose a tree to sleep in. In the day, he rode his horse slowly and carefully to avoid dangerous animals. He constantly looked around in search of the seven-colored bird. There were all kinds of birds and animals, some brightly colored, others not, but alas, there was no bird of seven colors. Finally, he rode out of the jungle, disappointed that he had not found what he had come for. He continued on his way until he reached a city surrounded by high walls.

At the gate of the city, there were many people coming and going, some who were young and in a hurry, and some who were old and walked at a slow pace. Outside of the city walls, the young prince saw an old haggard man, begging for his daily food. The kind-hearted prince gave the beggar some leftover food from his provisions and a few gold coins.

The old man was surprised to see such a good-hearted, generous person, and asked the prince, "What brought you here?" The young prince, not mentioning that he was a prince, told him that he was looking for a bird that could change to seven colors, sing seven songs, and dance seven dances.

The old man said, "You have come to the right place. There is a ruler in this city in a heavily guarded fortress. The exact bird you are looking for is imprisoned there in a golden cage. But beware! The ruler is very heartless and selfish. No one but him can come close to the bird."

The old man explained that he once lived in the fortress and served the ruler. He told the prince, "The ruler would punish and imprison a person for the slightest thing. One day, some of the servants and I, without reason, were harshly judged and sentenced to a lifetime in prison. I managed to escape. Since then, I have not stepped into the city for fear of being caught and thrown back in jail." He sadly told the prince that the bird had turned all grey because the mean ruler was unkind and always kept the poor creature locked up in its cage.

After the prince heard the old man's story, he entered the city and walked around the fortress, taking note of every detail. He sat down and planned how to free the bird. He went to the market and bought a rope, a hook, scissors, and some sticky dough. Then he bought a black and red outfit that looked like the uniform of a guard.

The following night he changed into the outfit to look like a guard. He left his horse near a tree in a dark corner near the fortress. He quickly climbed to the top of the fortress wall by rope and hook, and hid them in a corner for his return. Then, he boldly walked into the fortress, as if he had been a guard his whole life.

Shortly after, midnight arrived. Everyone in the fortress was fast sleep. Even the guards, who for years had not seen anyone with enough courage to get close to the fortress, dozed off at their posts. The prince quietly walked around the place, looking in every corner, and saw a dimly lit room. Lo and behold, there was the forlorn bird, sitting in a golden cage! The poor bird looked very sad. The prince quickly tiptoed towards the cage and talked to the bird softly, "Don't worry, dear bird, I have come to free you and take you to your partner." He opened the cage and explained to the bird how he planned their escape.

Now in those days, people had strings to tighten their pants instead of belts. So, when all of the guards were fast sleep, and all of the servants were snoring, and even the cruel ruler was deep in his dreams, the clever prince took his scissors and cut the ropes of their pants. Then, he took the sticky dough that he had bought in the market, and put a piece of dough under the soles of their shoes.

Using his rope and hook, he climbed down the wall with the bird flying after him.

One of the guards woke up and shouted, "Somebody is stealing the bird! Somebody is stealing the bird! Catch him! Catch him!" But, as soon as the sleepy guard stood up, his pants fell down! He pulled up his trousers and tried to put his shoes on, but they were firmly stuck to the floor. Then everyone in the court woke up and as soon as they got out of bed and stood up, their pants fell down, too. And no one could put on their shoes because they were all firmly stuck to the ground with dough. What a scene! Even the cruel ruler's pants fell down when he woke up, and even his shoes were stuck to the floor.

The prince mounted his trusty horse, and swiftly rode away with the bird flying close behind. They had made a daring escape from the heavily guarded fortress! They raced back through the jungle, over the mountainous roads and hills, to the fork in the road, and all the way back to the highway. After a few days of riding, the prince reached a place near his city and the royal castle.

The eldest brother, who had had enough of the good life in one of the cities, had come back to the same spot near the castle. He saw his younger brother riding towards the palace with the bird of seven colors on his shoulder and became jealous. "Why should he become king?" he thought to himself. "I am older and should rightfully take the throne."

He made a plan to take the bird away from his younger brother and claim the throne for himself. He approached the young prince and pretended to be very kind. "You look tired and should rest. Get off your horse, drink some water, and rest a little," he said. Then, he led his brother to a nearby well and told him, "Let me look after the bird while you draw some water and drink. We will both get refreshed and then go back home." But as soon as the younger brother started drawing some water, the mean older brother pushed him into the well. He snatched the bird, tied up its legs, and carried the poor thing away, riding speedily towards his father's palace.

When he reached the castle, he lied to his father and said, "I have gone a long way and through much hardship to find this bird. I deserve to be heir to the throne." The old man was happy to see that one of his sons had succeeded in bringing back a partner for his beloved bird. He planned a big celebration to pronounce his eldest son as the next king.

The servants took the newly arrived bird and put it close to the king's beloved seven-colored bird in the palace orchard. Everyone expected that the feathers of the king's bird would turn into seven beautiful colors, and sing seven beautiful songs, and dance seven wonderful dances. But both birds remained quiet, and the colors of both of their feathers were still all grey. They neither sang nor danced. The old king was puzzled, and summoned the wise man from his faraway village. The wise man proclaimed, "These birds sense injustice. Something wrong has happened."

The king sent his best soldiers to see if there were any injustices in his kingdom. The soldiers searched until they finally found the well with the young prince trapped deep inside. They pulled him out and listened to his story. The soldiers brought the young prince to the king, who was very happy to see him. The beloved son told his father all that had happened.

The king understood that choosing the eldest brother as the next king had been a mistake. The following morning, he gathered all the ministers, courtiers, and important people of the kingdom.

Then he invited all of his soldiers and servants. He told them about the terrible act of jealousy that the eldest prince had done. The old king decreed that the elder son would be banished from the palace forever, and pronounced the youngest prince as the rightful heir.

As soon as the youngest prince was pronounced heir to the throne, the two birds changed to seven beautiful colors, sang seven beautiful songs, and danced seven intricate dances. They remained loving soul mates for many, many years.

2

GreenRobe

Once upon a day and once upon a time, under the purple dome of the sky, there was an old woman who had a beautiful daughter called Ziba. They lived in a small village. Nearby, there was a river with a calm stream, whose water was crystal clear. The river was surrounded by large trees with beautiful branches full of green leaves.

Ziba and her mother took in clothes to wash for a living. They worked hard, scrubbing and washing and wringing the clothes at the river's edge, and then drying them in the hot sun. They earned little money, but were happy.

On top of one of the large green trees near the river, there was a tree house. There, lived a tall, handsome man called GreenRobe, who always wore green clothes and a long, flowing green robe. He would often pass by the river where Ziba and her mother washed clothes. Whenever he passed by, the old woman secretly wished that GreenRobe would ask for the hand of her daughter in marriage. But she soon put the thought away, thinking that they were much too poor for such a worthy match.

One day, GreenRobe walked towards Ziba's mother at the river bank. She thought that he wanted to have his green clothes washed, but instead, he asked for her daughter's hand in marriage! The old woman was very happy, as was her beautiful daughter.

Soon after, GreenRobe and Ziba were married. Many people came to their wedding. It was a huge and wonderful celebration, with guests from all over, who danced and clicked their heels to beautiful music until the light of dawn. The bride and groom danced around each other seven times, and each time they did so, their love for one another grew deeper and deeper.

GreenRobe and his new wife went to live in the tree house. It was a beautiful tree house with many rooms hidden in its trunk. As they entered their new home, GreenRobe turned to his new wife and said: "My darling Ziba, you and I will live happily in this tree house, but I must tell you something. There is a room that you must never enter, for if you do, I will never be able to return." Ziba promised that she would never open the forbidden room.

One day, while GreenRobe was at work, she found herself close to the forbidden room. The door was slightly ajar, and she thought to herself, "What is so special about this room? Why is it forbidden for me to see it?" She slowly pushed the door open, entered the dark room, peeked around, and quickly left.

GreenRobe did not come home from work that night, or the night after that, or the following night. In fact, there was no sign of him at all. Ziba cried and cried, and ran to tell her mother. On her way, she noticed that the cold autumn wind had caused all of the leaves to fall one by one.

Her mother said: "Oh, my poor dear girl! There is only one way to get your husband back. You must buy seven pairs of shoes made out of iron, and seven dresses made out of iron threads, and you must walk to seven distant cities until you wear out all seven pairs of iron shoes and all seven iron dresses. Only then will you find your GreenRobe again."

So, Ziba bought seven pairs of iron shoes and seven iron dresses, and started to walk. At first, her burdens were so heavy that she could barely put one foot in front of the other. And yet she kept going, slowly, with the heavy weight on her shoulders and a heavy heart. The winter cold added to her load. She walked and walked and walked until the winter snows came and went. She walked past villages, and she walked past cities, and she walked past forests.

Everywhere she went, she asked if anybody had seen or heard of her husband, GreenRobe. Some looked at her sympathetically, but didn't know the name or the dwelling place of GreenRobe. Others mocked and snickered and giggled and laughed at her behind her back. But she didn't care, and kept on walking in the hope of finding her dear lost husband. Her feet ached, and her shoulders ached, and her whole body ached, but still she walked on and on and on, through rain, through snow, through wind and cold, in search of her beloved GreenRobe.

Little by little, she felt her first pair of shoes wear out and her first iron dress droop. She changed to her second pair of iron shoes and a new iron dress, and continued to walk until she reached another city. And she walked on. Slowly, her second pair of shoes wore out, and her third, and her fourth. Gradually, her iron dresses became more faded and worn, and as she discarded each item, her pain became more bearable and her heart became lighter. And still she walked on.

One fine spring day, her seventh and last pair of shoes and her seventh and last iron dress wore out as she passed the seventh city. She came upon some vast green fields full of spring flowers and saw a farmer. "Have you seen my dear husband, GreenRobe?" she asked. The farmer answered, "These fields that you see all belong to the master, GreenRobe."

Ziba walked on and saw a shepherd with a flock of the finest sheep. "Do you know of my dear husband, GreenRobe?" she asked. The shepherd answered, "These fine sheep all belong to the master, GreenRobe."

Ziba started to run with excitement. She soon reached the most beautiful gardens filled with exquisite roses and fragrant jasmine and saw a gardener. "Do you know of my dear husband, GreenRobe?" she asked. The gardener looked up and said, "These gardens all belong to the master, GreenRobe." Ziba's eyes filled with tears of happiness.

Then Ziba reached a large castle. There, at its entrance, her beloved husband stood, waiting for her. She ran up the stairs straight into his arms. "I have waited for you for a long time," GreenRobe told her gently. "You have suffered greatly, but you are home with me now. I have seen your soul and felt your deep pain, but you will never suffer again."

They walked hand in hand into the castle, and all were happy to see the couple reunited in the deepest love possible.

3

The Silly Rooster

Once upon a day and once upon a time, under the purple dome of the sky, there was a rooster who was very mischievous and playful. He jumped up and down and bothered all of the hens. He constantly got into fights with all of the other roosters.

One day, he was acting up, and jumping up and down so much that he injured his back. The rooster's owner, who was a kind man, made some medicine out of seeds. He put some water on the seeds to make a paste, spread it on a piece of cloth, and wrapped it around the rooster's back.

The rooster got better but one of the seeds on his back started to sprout. It grew bigger and bigger until it became a large tree growing out of the rooster's back. Soon, the tree was so high that you could not see all of the leaves and branches at the top.

One day, the owner became very curious and decided to climb the tree to see what was there. When he reached the top branches of the tree, he saw an enormous watermelon. He took out his pocketknife to cut it open and eat. As he was cutting open the watermelon, his pocketknife fell inside the fruit. He put his hand into the watermelon to get his knife back, but as much as he tried, he did not succeed.

He decided to enter the watermelon to look for his missing knife. When he went inside, he saw a huge field. He looked everywhere, but there was no sign of his pocketknife, so he walked in farther to search some more.

In the distance, he saw some hills and a river where a number of people were also searching for something. He shouted to them, "Hey! Have you seen my pocketknife?" The people on the other side of the river seemed confused. He ran towards them. When he came closer, he asked them again, "Have you seen my pocketknife?"

They all laughed and laughed. When they could finally speak, they said, "Don't be silly! It's been a number of days that we have been looking for our lost camels. Do you expect to find your small pocketknife here?" They told the man to follow the river. "Maybe your knife has been carried away by the flow of the water," they suggested.

So, he walked along the river, hoping to find his pocketknife. After a long time, he reached a point where the river was dry. There, he saw an old, old woman fishing with a pole that had a line but no hook. She said to him, "Help me catch some fish and we will eat together."

They cast the line into the waterless river and caught a big fish. Then, they gathered a few pieces of wet wood and started a fire to cook. The flames of the fire reached the sky, but the pieces of wood did not burn. They found a frying pan without a bottom and put the fish inside. The old woman lifted the heavy pan onto the big flames. After frying a long time, the fish was still raw, but its bones were all burnt.

The old woman, who had no teeth, chewed the fish bones and became pregnant. Soon, she gave birth to three boys. The boys grew very quickly and learned how to talk.

The first boy said,

> *"I have a big head and my name is Kyu-kyu.*
> *I can pull all the meat off the hot barbeque."*

The second boy said,

> *"I am a hero, my name is Oof-oof.*
> *I can water the garden from the top of the roof."*

The third one said,

> *"I am wise and my name is Pell-beller.*
> *I am so clever and am the best seller."*

The old women complained about her plight to her sons and said,

> *"What shall we do? What shall we eat?*
> *So many children are under my feet!"*
> *No more food is coming our way.*
> *Nothing tomorrow, if we eat on this day,*
> *If we eat tomorrow, there's nothing today!"*

The old woman's sons thought about what to do.

> *Pell-beller said to the other three,*
> *"We'll pick some eggs from the big egg tree,*
> *On the donkey's back we'll load them for free,*
> *We won't sell to those who wish to buy,*
> *And to those who don't want, selling we'll try!"*
> *They loaded the eggs on their donkey's backs,*
> *And closed with strings, the brown gunnysacks.*

The three brothers reached the City of Bragg. They sought a customer to buy their eggs. As they looked around, they saw many strange things.

> *This is what they saw in the City of Bragg,*
> *A donkey made carpets of felt from a rag,*
> *The grocery store was owned by a cat,*
> *The dog had a butcher shop where all day he sat,*
> *A feisty mosquito built homes for a rat.*
> *He fell off the roof, and was buried beneath,*
> *And broke every one of his seventy teeth.*

Finally, they found a customer for their eggs.

> *There was a raven, with no work to do,*
> *And into the City of Bragg, she flew.*
> *She bought the eggs and on them she sat,*
> *And forty ravens she begat.*
> *The people of Bragg, they heard this strange story,*
> *Like gossipers' rumors, that one could make forty.*

After the three brothers sold all of the eggs to the raven, they became very rich and returned to their old mother. The owner of the rooster came down from the tree, and once in a while, in the watermelon season, went to visit the old woman and her three sons. The raven liked the City of Bragg and stayed there forever.

> *Now our story's been told to the end,*
> *But the raven never returned home, my friend.*

4

Beebee Chaghzeh

Once upon a day and once upon a time, under the purple dome of the sky, there lived a mother with her three daughters. They were all very good, and beautiful, and smart. But the youngest one was the cleverest of all. Ever since she was a little girl, her sisters called her Beebee Chaghzeh; "Beebee", or grandmother, because she had the wisdom of a grandmother, and "Chaghzeh", or toad, because she was always jumping from one place to another like a toad.

Every night, before going to sleep, their mother told them stories. Soon, everyone fell asleep, except for Beebee Chaghzeh. The mother would ask,

"Who is asleep? Who is awake?"

And Beebee Chaghzeh would answer,

"Everyone is asleep. Beebee Chaghzeh is awake!"

Beebee Chaghzeh would lay awake and think about all the things she had learned that day, and plan what to do the next day.

One night, Beebee Chaghzeh's tired mother fell into a deep sleep after she had told her last story. The other sisters were all sound asleep, but Beebee Chaghzeh was still awake. The restless girl lay in bed, and tossed and turned. Without knowing why, she felt very worried.

Then, she heard a faint and unfamiliar sound of someone tiptoeing through the house. She turned over in bed so that she could see the door. "Someone is in the courtyard and coming close to the room," she thought to herself. The sound of the footsteps became louder and louder. Before she knew it, Beebee Chaghzeh saw an ugly witch open the door, and come straight into the room!

The witch muttered under her breath, "Now is the time I can take these beautiful girls with their mother, and turn them all into witches as my helpers." She cast a spell and chanted,

> *"All who are asleep, asleep you shall stay,*
> *Until I shall take my spell away!"*

Beebee Chaghzeh was awake and the spell did not affect her. She was very frightened but kept her wits about her. Pretending to be asleep, she looked around the room with her eyes half-opened and thought to herself "I must find a way to get rid of this wicked witch!"

The witch carried them all one by one into her large dark carriage. Inside, there were shelves with books of witchcraft, and a long tabletop covered with glass jars and all sorts of strange vials. The carriage was like a room, and had a window at the back and a window at the front.

The witch pulled the reins of the carriage, and the fearful horses galloped towards her dark and mighty fortress. Every now and again, she looked back through the front window to make sure that everyone was still under her spell. The carriage got closer and closer to the witch's palace, and clever Beebee Chaghzeh pretended that she was still fast asleep.

The carriage came to a stop, and the witch got out to open the big gate of her dreaded fortress. Beebee Chaghzeh saw her chance. She quickly climbed out of the small front window of the carriage, and jumped into the driver's seat. Grabbing the reins, she gently turned the horses around to go back home. The horses, which hated the rough ways of the wicked witch, felt the gentle touch of Beebee Chaghzeh. They readily galloped away from the fortress in the hope of being set free.

When the witch realized that someone had stolen her precious carriage, she started to run after it, shaking her clenched hands and shrieking in a horrible witch's voice, "Stop! Stop the carriage! If you don't and I catch you, I will turn the biggest part of your body into your ear!"

Beebee Chaghzeh heard the witch's curse and quickly jumped back into the carriage. She looked out the back window and saw the ugly witch running behind. The clever girl took all of the glass bottles filled with potions and dropped them onto the road. They broke into a thousand pieces. The witch didn't give up the chase, and ran through the broken glass, which pierced her shoes and cut the soles of her feet.

"Ow, oow, ouch!" the witch cried out. She was very angry and her feet hurt very much. The wicked witch sat down on the side of the road, and took off her shoes to remove the glass pieces from her feet. Beebee Chaghzeh saw that the witch had stopped chasing the carriage and cried out gently to the horses, "Faster! Faster!" The horses listened to her, and ran faster on their own, even though Beebee Chaghzeh wasn't holding the reins.

But the witch was a witch and knew a lot of magic tricks. She took out her wand, said a few incantations, and magically jumped over the remaining pieces of glass. The nasty, wicked witch got closer and closer to the carriage.

Clever Beebee Chaghzeh saw the witch getting closer and closer. She eyed a jar full of sharp pins and needles. She grabbed the jar and emptied it onto the road. The wicked witch ran over the sharp pins and needles. They pierced her shoes and pricked the soles of her feet, hurting them even more.

"Ow, oow, ouch!" the witch cried out. Her feet hurt so much that she had to sit down on the side of the road to pull out all of the sharp pins and needles.

But the witch was a witch and knew a lot of magic tricks. She took out her wand, said a few incantations, and magically jumped over the remaining pins and needles. The witch got closer and closer to the carriage.

Clever Beebee Chaghzeh saw the witch getting closer and closer. She looked around the carriage and found some bags of salt and hot Indian pepper. She opened the bags and poured out the salt and pepper onto the road. As the witch ran, her shoes became filled with the salt and hot pepper. This made her really angry because her feet started burning.

"Ow, oow, ouch!" the witch cried out. She could stand it no longer. The wicked witch sat by the side of the road and took her shoes off to attend to her aching, burning feet. She was in such pain that she could not remember any of her magic incantations. The witch had finally given up chasing the carriage.

Then, Beebee Chaghzeh flung out all the books of witchcraft onto every corner of the road. The sun was beginning to rise from the east when the carriage reached Beebee Chaghzeh's house. She awakened her sleeping mother and sisters, and told them what had happened. They cried in joy and said, "Clever girl! You have freed us all!"

Morning arrived and the sun was burning brightly in the sky. The witch came to collect her books, but saw that people had already picked them up and could read all of her evil spells. All her treacherous secrets were now revealed! The witch ran away and was never seen again.

Beebee Chaghzeh told the horses that they were free and could go wherever they chose. The horses were very happy to be away from the wicked witch and gladly stayed with Beebee Chaghzeh.

They all lived happily ever after. Beebee Chaghzeh grew up and one day became a real "Beebee!"

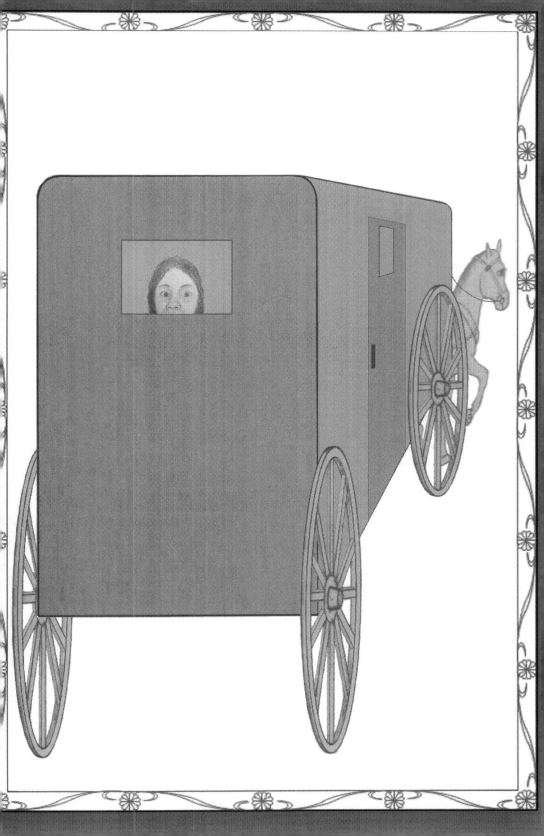

5

The Little Wooden Horse

Once upon a day and once upon a time, under the purple dome of the sky, there was an old king whose greatest wish was to see his only son get married and rule after him. One day, the prince disguised himself as a simple man and went to the city. It was his first time outside of the palace walls. He was very curious and walked around to see how ordinary people lived.

By chance, he passed by a house and looked through the window, and saw three beautiful sisters talking among themselves. The prince was amazed by their beauty. The eldest sister said, "If I were to marry the prince, I would knit him a light blanket that is warm in winter, cool in summer, and so thin that it could be folded up and fit into a walnut shell." The second sister said, "If I were to marry the prince, I would sew him a light suit that never needs to be washed or ironed, and is comfortable in winter and summer. The youngest sister said, "It I were to marry the prince, I would bear twins – a boy with golden hair, and a girl with pearls woven into her braids.

The prince returned to the palace and told his father, "I have seen three beautiful sisters and I wish to marry them all." The king was very happy and ordered his aides to go into the city, find the house where the three sisters lived, and bring them back to the palace. And so, it was done. The king arranged a big wedding, and the three sisters were wed to the prince. A few months after the wedding, the old king died. The prince sat on the royal throne and became the new ruler.

After some time, the young king asked the eldest sister, "Have you made the blanket that you promised to knit for me?" She answered, "I am working on it, but it will take some time." Then he asked the second sister, "Have you made the suit that you promised to sew for me?" She answered, "I am sewing it, but it will take some time." Then he asked the youngest sister, "When will you give birth to a boy with golden hair, and a girl with pearls woven into her braids?" She answered, "I am pregnant, and by the end of the year, the twins will be born."

In the coming weeks and months, the young king asked the three sisters the same questions and received the same answers. The king became annoyed at this. He did not know that the two elder sisters were lying to him and had made false promises. But his youngest wife was indeed pregnant, and by the end of the year, gave birth to twins – a boy with golden hair, and a girl with pearls woven into her braids.

The two older sisters, who had made false promises, became very jealous of the youngest sister, who had kept her word. The older sisters were afraid that the king would find out that they had lied, and throw them out of the palace. They went to their youngest sister and pretended to help her. Each one took a baby and told the younger sister, "You have just had these babies and need some rest. You can sleep and we will take good care of your twins."

They took the babies and rushed to the king and said, "Dear King! We have kept our promise and brought you a boy with golden hair, and a girl with pearls woven into her braids." The king turned to the older sister and said, "But you promised me a light blanket that is warm in winter, cool in summer, and so thin that it could be folded up and fit into a walnut shell." Then he turned to the second sister and said, "And you promised me a light suit that never needs to be washed or ironed, and is comfortable in winter and summer."

The sisters answered, "No, our youngest sister could not keep her promise, and told us that she would make the blanket and the suit. Instead, one of us would give birth to a boy with golden hair, and the other would give birth to a girl with pearls woven into her braids."

The king, believing the two jealous sisters, became angry at his youngest wife, and ordered her to be put in prison. The courtiers, who knew the true story, said among themselves, "The two elder sisters have deceived the king. Let us hide this young mother of twins somewhere in the palace. Hopefully, one day the king will understand the truth."

The palace was very big. It had a large garden that was full of beautiful trees and flowers. At the other side of the garden, there was a building where all of the cooks and servants of the palace lived. The courtiers found a room with a window overlooking the gardens, and hid the young queen there. "Dear lady," they said. "The king has ordered us to put you in prison. But we know that you are innocent and have kept your promise to the king. Never leave this room so we can tell the king that we have done our duty."

Years passed by, and the twins became older. They were particularly clever and curious. They liked to go everywhere in the palace and discover every room and every corner. One day, they came to the far side of the garden to the servants' quarters. There, behind the window, they were surprised to see a beautiful woman. They felt a great sense of love for her, as though they had known her for many years. Their mother immediately recognized the boy with the golden hair and the girl with the pearls woven into her braids as her own children, and she wept with joy.

The children shyly came close to her window. "Who are you?" they asked. "I am someone who loves you very much," she answered. She asked them to come and see her every day. The twins, feeling her love, came to see her every day. They asked, "Why don't you ever come out of this room? Please, won't you come visit us in the palace?" Their mother told them, "If you want me to come to the palace, ask your father to buy you a little wooden horse."

The children went to their father and asked him to buy them a little wooden horse. The king, who loved his children, told his servants to buy them a beautiful wooden horse. That day, the children came to see their mother, and brought the wooden horse to show her. The mother said, "Now go to the cooks and ask for a bowl of oats." And so they did. Then she told them to sit down in front of the king and say over and over again,

> *"Little wooden horsey, eat oats, eat oats!*
> *Little wooden horsey, eat oats!"*

The mother continued, "If the king says that wooden horses can't eat oats, ask him how women who are not pregnant can bear babies."

The twins went back to the palace. At lunchtime, they put the wooden horse on the table with a bowl of oats in front of it. They said over and over again,

> *"Little wooden horsey, eat oats, eat oats!*
> *Little wooden horsey, eat oats!"*

The king asked them to be quiet and eat their food. But they continued, and repeatedly said,

> *"Little wooden horsey, eat oats, eat oats!*
> *Little wooden horsey, eat oats!"*

The king became angry and shouted, "But wooden horses can't eat oats!" And then they replied, "If wooden horses can't eat oats, how can women who are not pregnant bear babies?"

The king asked his children, "Who taught you this?" The twins replied, "There is a loving and kind woman at the far corner of the palace where the cooks and servants live. She never comes out of her room, even though we have asked her many times to come visit us in the palace."

The king realized that the kind lady must be his youngest wife, and understood that he had made a terrible mistake. He ordered the two older jealous sisters to be sent out of the palace, and brought his youngest wife back to her rightful place to be the only queen. They all lived happily in the palace for many years, but the little wooden horse never ate oats.

6

The Magic Zucchini

O nce upon a day and once upon a time, under the purple dome of the sky, there lived a young man called Morad. He had old parents, who were very poor. Morad diligently took care of his parents, and worked very hard on the family farm so that they would have enough food to eat. Every day, after returning from the farm, he cooked for his old parents, prepared the table for supper, and cleaned the house. At the end of the day, he would slump down in a corner and rest before finally going to bed. But he never complained.

One day, a fairy saw Morad's plight and appeared to him while he was working hard on the farm. The fairy said to him, "You are helping everybody so much and carrying such a heavy load. I will give you four presents to help you:

The first present is a zucchini plant. Take care of it and water it and it will provide you with a new ripe zucchini every day. When you cook the zucchini, it will taste like anything you wish.

The second present is a hen that lays an egg every day. But once a year in spring, on the day of Nowruz, it will lay a golden egg.

The third present is a donkey that can run very fast in times of need.

The fourth present is a magic stick that will take care of you. Should anyone wish to harm you or your family, the magic stick will help you."

The fairy looked at Morad and warned, "You must promise to never stop working hard, or become lazy, or care only for yourself." Morad couldn't believe his good fortune. He thanked the fairy many times and promised that he would never stop working hard, or become self-indulgent and lazy.

Every day, Morad watered and tended the magic plant, and it gave forth a new ripe zucchini. Morad cooked the zucchini and it would taste like anything that they wished to eat. And every day, the hen laid a fresh farm egg. So the family never went hungry, and Morad did not have to work so hard in the fields.

On Nowruz of that year, the hen laid a large, golden egg. Morad took it to a trustworthy goldsmith, and sold it for a hefty price, and they were poor no longer. Now it was very easy to care for his old parents.

The year after, on Nowruz, the hen laid another golden egg. Morad became very wealthy, and little by little stopped working on the farm. Most of the time, he stayed at home in bed and ate a lot of food and sweets. Soon, he became very fat and lazy.

The story of the golden egg reached the ears of many people. A thief decided to find out if there was indeed a golden egg on Morad's farm. For many days and months, he sneaked around the farm and noticed that Morad paid particular attention to a particular hen. Finally, it was the day of Nowruz. The thief, hiding in a corner, saw the hen laying the golden egg. Morad, who had become careless and lazy, casually put the egg in his pocket and went to sleep under a tree.

The thief crept past the sleeping man. Just as he reached for the egg in Morad's pocket, the thief thought to himself, "If I only steal the egg, I will get money now, but if I steal the egg and the hen, I will get money now and have money forevermore." So, he stole both the egg and the hen, and quickly ran away.

When Morad woke up, he realized that his egg was missing. He went back to the house without even checking the coop. He was so groggy that he fell into bed and went back to sleep. Then he heard a knock at the door. "Knock, knock, knock." He turned over, hoping that whoever was knocking would go away. Alas, the knocking became louder and louder. Morad stood up to see who was at the door. To his surprise, he saw that it was the magic stick.

The magic stick flew up and pointed towards the farm. Morad opened the door and followed the magic stick to the chicken coop. To his horror, he saw that the magic hen had also been stolen. Upset and saddened, Morad realized that he had not kept his promise to the fairy. His shoulders slumped, his head drooped down, one hand clutched the other, and he started to moan.

The magic stick tapped Morad gently on the back a number of times. Irritated, Morad looked up and said, "What do you want from my life?" The magic stick pointed towards the donkey. The donkey started to bray and stomp its feet as if to say, "I'm ready to run!" Morad jumped on the donkey's back. It ran swiftly, following the stick that was flying ahead.

Finally, the magic stick stopped at the thief's house, and the donkey stopped right behind. The magic stick flew to the thief's door and knocked loudly. "Knock, knock, knock!" The thief hoped that whoever was knocking would go away. But the knocking became louder and louder. The thief opened the door to see what was happening.

Morad told the thief, "We have come to retrieve the golden egg and the hen that you have stolen from us!" The thief pretended not to understand and asked, "Which hen?" The magic stick flew inside, found the hen, and tapped it on its legs gently, forcing it to run outside the house. The startled thief lied, "I was working around your farm. It seems that your hen followed me back home without me knowing it. As for a golden egg, I don't know what you are talking about."

The magic stick flew behind the thief and spanked him soundly on his behind. "Ouch, ouch!" said the thief, putting his hands behind his back and rubbing his bottom. He ran inside the house, put the golden egg into his pocket, mounted his horse, and started to run away. "They will never catch me on my fast horse," thought the thief.

Morad, who was still on the donkey, tapped his shoes on the donkey's sides. The hen jumped on the donkey's back and sat in front of Morad. In this time of need, the donkey ran faster than ever, even faster than the horse. It soon caught up to the thief and blocked his way.

The magic stick flew in front of the thief and wagged itself up and down like a stern finger. The frightened thief realized that he wouldn't be able to keep the stolen egg. He took it out of his pocket and threw it down to the ground. Morad, who was happy to get his egg and hen back, let the thief go.

From that day on, Morad kept his promise to the fairy. He worked hard in the fields, but not too hard. Every Nowruz, the hen laid a golden egg. Morad sold it well, and helped not only his parents but all of the needy. The zucchini plant provided a new ripe zucchini every day, and Morad and his parents ate delicious meals for many, many years to come. As for the magic stick, it sometimes got bored and drummed on the kitchen pots and pans, and once in a while, it chased the donkey just for fun.

7

Shangol, Mangol and Dastegol

Once upon a day and once upon a time, under the purple dome of the sky, there was a goat with three little kids. One little kid was called Shangol, one was called Mangol, and the third was called Dastegol.

One day, the mother goat had to go out of the house to get food. She told her three little kids, "I am going to bring food for everybody. After I am gone, keep the door closed and latch it. Don't open the door for anyone but me, and don't let any stranger inside of the house. If someone knocks, before opening the door, look through the peephole and make sure that it is me. Watch carefully and see my four henna-colored red paws and long white beard. And listen carefully to make sure that it is my sweet voice and no one else's." The mother goat went out of the house with her saddlebag, and carefully closed the door behind her. The little kids dutifully locked the big wooden latch.

After the mother goat left, a wolf came and knocked on the door. The kids asked, "Who is there?" The wolf answered, "Open the door. I am your mother and I have brought you food." The kids looked through the peephole in the door and said, "You are not our mother. Her paws are henna red!" The wolf went and put henna on its paws to make them look all red.

The bad wolf came back to the house and again knocked on the door. The kids asked, "Who is there?" The wolf answered, "Open the door. I am your mother and I have brought you food." The kids looked through the peephole in the door and shouted, "You are not our mother. She has a long white beard!" The wolf went to stick some white wool on its chin.

The wolf returned to the goat's house, and knocked on the door again. The kids asked, "Who is there?" The wolf answered, "Open the door. I am your mother and I have brought you food." The three little kids looked through the peephole and said, "You do not sound like our mother. Her voice is kind and sweet!" The wolf coughed and said, "I have a sore throat. Look! My paws are red and I have a long white beard."

Shangol did not want to open the door. Mangol said, "Maybe it is our mother." Little Dastegol cried, "Mommy! Mommy!" and rushed to the door and unlatched it. As soon as the door was opened, the bad wolf came in and swallowed Shangol and Mangol and Dastegol!

The mother goat came back and found the door open. The house was empty and her three little kids were gone! She cried aloud,

> *"Who ate up my Shangol?*
> *Who ate up my Mangol?*
> *Who ate up my Dastegol?*
> *Whoever ate them up I dare,*
> *Will fight against my horn, I swear!"*

She smelled her way towards the bad wolf, which had eaten so much that it couldn't even walk. The wolf rolled over and groaned, and the mother goat saw that its stomach was very large, and there were little goat hooves kicking from inside. The wolf grinned and said:

> *"I ate up your Shangol!*
> *I ate up your Mangol!*
> *I ate up your Dastegol!"*

The mother goat used her horn to rip the wolf's stomach open and freed her three small goats. The three little kids jumped up and down, and were very happy to see their mother.

The sore wolf left, hardly able to walk, and took a long time to recover. From that day on, Shangol, Mangol and Dastegol never opened the door again for anybody but their mother.

8

The Prince and the Goat

Once upon a day and once upon a time, under the purple dome of the sky, there lived a king who had no children. After many years, when he was already rather old, his wife gave birth to a beautiful boy. The king had a younger, jealous brother, who wanted to take over his kingdom and sit on the throne. When the young prince was born, the younger brother lost hope of ever ruling, and his jealousy reached new heights.

The old king became sick and knew that there was not much left of his time on earth. He called his most trusted advisors, and told them to protect his newborn son. When he passed away, the king's younger brother seized the throne. He ordered his soldiers to take the prince away from the palace and kill him.

The trusted courtiers of the late king took the newborn prince and wrapped him in a warm shawl. They gave the swaddled infant to a skilled horseman. The worthy horseman took the baby prince to a faraway village in the high mountains, and gave him to a kind and trustworthy nanny.

Meanwhile, the faithful courtiers took a small goat, wrapped it in a shawl, and gave it to a group of horsemen to ride out in the opposite direction. The riders reached a village and found a dry well. They threw the poor goat inside.

The village fool was passing by and saw them. He asked, "Why are all of you gathered around the well?" They answered, "We threw the baby prince inside, on order of the new king."

The riders, fearful of the new king, did not return to the palace. Each one rode away in his own direction.

The courtiers told the king that they had done his bidding and had made sure that the prince had been thrown into a well. But the king was very suspicious and sent soldiers to check if indeed the prince was dead. The soldiers searched for many days in many corners of the land. They announced, "The prince has been stolen! Has anyone seen the baby prince being carried away?" But no one had seen the wrapped up prince.

Eventually, the king's soldiers came to the village of the fool. The villagers said, "We haven't seen anyone." But the village fool came forward and insisted, "The prince was thrown into the well, by order of the new king." The soldiers asked the fool to lead them to the well. They tied a rope around the fool's waist and lowered him down into the well. "When you reach the bottom, take the prince and we will pull you up," they told him.

When the fool reached the bottom of the well, he saw the goat and shouted back,

"Your prince, he has a horn?"

The soldiers laughed at him and answered, "No, look better!" The fool looked at the goat and shouted up to the soldiers,

> *"Your prince, he has a beard and fluffy wool?"*

They answered back, "No, look better!" The fool asked,

> *"Your prince, he has a tail?"*

They answered back, "No, bring us the prince already!" The fool grabbed the goat. He tugged on the rope and the soldiers pulled him up.

They took the goat from the fool and wrapped it up carefully in the shawl. On their way out of the village, they cried tearfully so that all of the villagers could hear them, "We found the dear prince dead in a well."

The fool told the villagers, "The prince has a horn, and a tail, and a beard, and fluffy wool!" But everyone just laughed at him.

On the way back, the head soldier warned, "We must all swear that the prince is dead, or our new king will be very angry and kill us." When the soldiers returned to the palace, they all swore to the king that they had found the prince dead in a well.

Meanwhile, the baby prince grew up in the faraway village high up in the mountains with his kind and trusted nanny. He had now become a strong and courageous young man who could lead others. He rode horses better than anyone and was a highly skilled bowman. More importantly, he grew to be a kind and gentle soul whom everyone loved.

The trusted men of the late king, who had watched the prince grow up, decided that he was now old enough to know the true story of his birthright. They told him how his jealous uncle had unrightfully taken the throne. Then, they helped him gather a fine army in order to return to the palace.

The prince and his trusted army finally reached the palace gates. The head soldier cried out, "We have brought the true king back to the palace. He is the son of the late king, alive and well!" When the prince's uncle heard these words, he fled in fear into the depths of the forest, never to be heard of again.

9

The Citron Princess

Once upon a day and once upon a time, under the purple dome of the sky, there was a very beautiful kingdom called the Land of Citron. In the middle of the land, there was a big river with crystal clear water, and a stream so gentle that its surface looked like a mirror. The land was full of citron trees, which mainly grew near the river. The leaves of the trees were a deep shade of green, and the branches were laden with lemony citrons that had thick yellow skins.

The king of the Land of Citron was a kind and gentle soul. He had a lovely wife and a graceful daughter, whose beauty was known throughout the land. He loved his family and his people, and was concerned about their safety and well-being.

In a small hut near the river, there lived an ugly, mean-spirited witch. She was very jealous of the king, and his lovely queen, and their beautiful daughter. One day, the witch used her black magic and suddenly appeared in the palace. She brazenly faced the king and said, "I want to marry you and be the Queen of the Land of Citron!" The king replied, "I am happily married and love my wife and daughter." The witch flew into a terrible rage. She vowed to take revenge as she left the palace, screaming and shouting.

That evening, the mean witch concocted magic potions and recited evil incantations. As the full moon appeared overhead, she cackled and struck her wand on one of the bottles filled with potion, and said,

> *"Before, you were happy in the palace afar,*
> *Tonight, you are here, in citrons you are!"*

The evil witch imprisoned the queen and her daughter inside two large citrons. Then she hit the magic bottle once more. The two citrons were now hanging from a high branch of a tree near the river.

The morning after, the king woke up and found that his beloved wife and daughter were missing. He sent his soldiers to find the queen and the princess, but alas, there was no sign of them anywhere. He became very sad. The people in the Land of Citron became dispirited and cried bitterly. A blanket of melancholy covered the kingdom that colored it with shades of lamentation. The deep spell of sadness seeped through the hearts of all. No laughter was heard. No songs were sung. Even the birds in the sky were sorrowful and forlorn. The witch saw that all of the people and all of the creatures in the kingdom had become unhappy, and felt joy in their misery.

Every morning, the witch woke up and went to the river to wash up. She looked at the surface of the clear, calm water. The beauty of the princess was so strong that it radiated outward from the citron and was reflected by the water. The witch, who only loved herself, mistook the beautiful reflection as her own. She muttered to herself,

> *"I am so beautiful, I am so dear,*
> *One day, a queen, I will be here!"*

The princess heard the witch's self-admiring incantation through the thick skin of the citron and began to laugh. Her laughter, like her beauty, emanated from the fruit and fell upon the ears of the witch. The witch screamed angrily, "Quiet! Quiet!" The princess laughed and said,

> *"You evil witch, just go away,*
> *The king, he hates you every day!"*

The witch became very angry and threw a stone at the citron. The fruit broke off and fell into the river. The queen mother, still imprisoned in the citron fruit hanging from the tree, was now alone. From within the citron she cried,

> *"My beautiful girl, my beautiful daughter,*
> *Who will save you from the depths of the water?"*

Nobody but the witch heard her cries. The citron with the entrapped princess fell into the water's depths. Suddenly, a big red fish came up and swallowed it whole. The fish swam down the river with the citron fruit in its now enlarged belly. Within the deep calm river, it swam farther and farther away until it reached a distant kingdom.

In the kingdom, there was a king who loved his only son very much. The prince was handsome, and strong, and fearless. One day, the prince became very ill. His father was distraught and called the best doctors to find a cure. A wise old doctor came to the palace and said, "The cure for your son's illness is a dish made from a rare red fish that can only be found in the depths of the river."

The king summoned the best fishermen in the land to catch such a fish. The hand of fate brought the big red fish with the entrapped citron into the net of a skillful fisherman. The fish was carried into the kitchen of the castle. As soon as the cook picked up a knife to clean it, he heard a voice from within:

"Use the blade, wise and slow,
Peel each layer as you go."

The cook was startled and thought that perhaps he had just imagined it all. So, he called one of his helpers. His assistant cook raised the knife, and as soon as he did so, heard the same words.

The frightened cook went to the king, who was busy attending his sick son, and told him of the strange event. Before the king had a chance to say anything, the prince suddenly got out of bed and went to the kitchen. He picked up the knife to clean the fish and heard the words:

"Use the blade, wise and slow,
Peel each layer as you go."

The prince thought to himself, "What a beautiful and lovely voice." Hearing the words, he suddenly gained strength, and soon felt so well that there was no trace of his illness. The prince said in a strong, clear voice,

"Let no fear come into your heart,
With care I'll take the fish apart."

He skillfully cut the fish open, and to his surprise, saw the citron. He took out the valuable fruit and heard the same beautiful voice.

He washed the citron, took a small knife, and carefully removed the skin layer by layer. As the prince peeled off the citron rind, the witch's magic became weaker and weaker. Eventually, the evil magic was there no longer and lo and behold, the beautiful princess emerged. The prince was amazed to see such a beautiful young woman. He immediately fell in love with her, and she with him. The princess told him all that had happened. She begged the prince to help free her mother from the citron, and free her land from the clutches of the wicked witch. "Only a fearless, pure-hearted person like you can undo the witch's magic," she told the prince.

The prince gathered a group of skillful warriors and along with the princess, journeyed to the Land of Citron. They rode along the river until they came near the witch's hut. The prince told them to hide among the trees. Soon after, the prince spotted the witch near the river and said to his soldiers, "While I distract her, sneak into her hut and break all of the jars full of magic potions."

The prince walked towards the witch. He saw two images in the mirror-like river, the radiant face of the beautiful queen, and the ugly reflection of her evil face. He said to the self-admiring witch, "What a beautiful image. What is the secret of this beauty?" She flirted back, "It is my beauty. When I come near the water, the birds sing and the flowers blossom." While the witch continued extolling her virtues, the soldiers entered her hut and broke all of the bottles and jars that were full of potions. As soon as they did, she fell to the ground, losing all of her evil powers. The ugly reflection of the witch disappeared completely from the surface of the water.

Looking up from the queen's beautiful image in the water, the prince could see the citron in which she was imprisoned. A soldier climbed up the tree, picked the citron, and handed it to the prince. The prince took out his knife to open the citron, and heard her kind voice from within,

> *"Use the blade, wise and slow,*
> *Peel each layer as you go."*

The prince peeled the citron very carefully, as he had done for the princess, until the queen emerged. The princess and her mother were happily reunited and the witch's evil magic spell was broken forever.

The prince and his soldiers escorted the queen and the princess back to their palace. The color of lamentation had disappeared from the land. The people were at the height of happiness and joy. Laughter was heard once more. Songs were sung. Even the birds rose up and swooped with glee in the clear blue sky. The prince married the princess and they lived happily ever after. As for the mean witch, she was never seen in the Land of Citron again.

10

Hassan Ali

Once upon a day and once upon a time, under the purple dome of the sky, there was a beautiful and fearless princess called Mastaneh. She was the most skillful horsewoman and archer in the palace. Mastaneh fell in love with Hassan Ali, the son of the prime minister, but the king was very unhappy about this.

Mastaneh begged her father to let her marry Hassan Ali, but the King refused. This made Mastaneh very angry and upset. The princess was so much in love with Hassan Ali that she decided to leave the palace and marry him without her father's consent. Mastaneh met Hassan Ali and told him about her plan to escape. She said, "One night, you and I will each mount a horse and ride out of the city. We will meet in a faraway place near the river. The day after, without my father's permission, we shall marry."

On the night of their escape, Mastaneh mounted her horse and left the palace, bravely riding out in the middle of the dark night. She rode for a long time. As far as the eye could see, there was the darkness of the night, and as far as the ear could hear, there was only the sound of howling jackals. Far away, she saw a flickering light.

Mastaneh continued riding fearlessly until she reached the planned meeting place near the river. She whispered, "Hassan Ali," but there was no answer. She said a bit louder, "Hassan Ali." Still there was no answer. Finally, she angrily shouted, "Hassan Ali!" This time a sleepy voice answered, "Yes, what do you want?" She responded, "Have you forgotten that we were to meet here and continue with our plans?" The sleepy voice answered, "Whatever you say, my lady. Can you kindly let me sleep? I am extremely tired. Please, find a corner to sleep and tomorrow I will do whatever you wish." Mastaneh, exhausted and irritated by the strange behavior of Hassan Ali, found a nearby corner to fall sleep.

When the sun rose in the morning, Mastaneh woke up but she didn't see Hassan Ali. Irritated, she shouted, "Hassan Ali! Where are you?" After a short time, a young man in dusty clothes appeared and quickly came forward. He said, "My lady, what is it that you want?" Surprised and scared, Mastaneh looked at him and said haughtily, "Get away from me! Who are you?" The young man replied politely, "My lady, my name is Hassan Ali. I am a shepherd here."

Mastaneh realized that Hassan Ali, the son of the prime minister, was so fearful of the king that he had not even left the palace. Disappointed at his behavior, she didn't know what to do. She thought, "This young shepherd is polite and seems reliable. It is better to have him accompany me until I decide my next move." Mastaneh asked the young man, "Can you ride your horse beside mine along the river?" The shepherd answered, "Surely, my lady. Please give me a moment to wash up."

The shepherd went to wash up behind a tree near the river. He changed into clean clothes that he had taken from his bundle and combed his hair. Then, he returned to the princess, who was sitting and waiting for him. Now that he was nice and clean, the princess saw that he was actually a handsome young man. The shepherd brought out some bread and cheese for breakfast, and they sat down to eat.

After breakfast, they started riding their horses along the river. As they were going, they saw giant ants carrying large rubies to their nest. The shepherd was very surprised to see such a thing. He got off of his horse and started collecting some of the jewels. Mastaneh told Hassan Ali, "Let us see where these rubies come from and who they belong to." Hassan Ali remounted his horse and they followed the long line of ants.

After riding for some time, they reached a high wall. There, the ants were coming out of a small hole at the bottom of the wall. Hassan Ali said to Mastaneh, "My lady, I shall go to the other side of this wall in order to find the secret of these rubies." The princess nodded and said, "You need not say 'my lady' all the time. You may call me by my name, Mastaneh."

Hassan Ali told Mastaneh, "There is an abandoned hut nearby. If I don't come back before dark, sleep there tonight. Tomorrow morning, come back to this wall to see if I have returned. If you don't see me by the end of the day, go your own way." Mastaneh said that she would wait for him near the wall, and cautioned him to be careful.

Hassan Ali climbed over the high wall and entered a large courtyard. He followed the ants until he reached a pond. Water poured in at one side and flowed into a small stream at the other. Near the pond there was a big tree. Every few seconds, a small drop of blood fell into the pond from the tree and turned into a ruby. The tree's branches were tangled and had many leaves, so Hassan Ali could not see exactly where the drops of blood were coming from. The stream of water carried so many rubies away that some had piled up onto its sides. From there, the ants took the gems and carried them back to their nest.

Within the walls surrounding the courtyard, Hassan Ali could see a huge gate. In the middle of the courtyard, there was a large house that had a very big door and very big windows. The sun was setting and it was getting darker and darker. A sudden fear befell him, though he didn't know why. He decided to climb a high tree farther away from the pond and hide there. "Tomorrow, when the sun rises, I will continue my search," he thought to himself. He climbed the tree and kept watch over the pond as he hid himself among the intertwined branches.

Soon after, a huge and ugly ghoul entered the gate of the courtyard and roared like thunder,

> *"I scream and shout,*
> *I smell a human about."*

The ghoul angrily looked around and stomped towards the pond. He came near the tree that had the dripping blood. From it, he snatched the head of a beautiful girl from one of its branches and took her body from another. Then, the ugly ghoul lifted a stone from a corner of the pond and took out a jar. He opened it and poured its elixir into the palm of his hand. Then he used the elixir to connect the girl's head to her body.

From his hiding place, Hassan Ali saw the young girl come back to life. She was very beautiful, but looked so sad. The ill-tempered and heartless ghoul ordered her to fetch him food and drink. After the young girl cleaned and tidied up, the ghoul grabbed her and carried her off into the big house.

The next morning, Hassan Ali saw the ghoul separating the girl's head from her body and hiding each part in a different branch of the tree. Then, the ghoul left. Soon after, Hassan Ali scrambled down the tree where he had been hiding. He climbed up the tree near the pond, and took down the girl's head and her body. Then, he found the jar with the magic elixir, opened it up, and put the girl back together.

When she opened her eyes, she was surprised to see Hassan Ali instead of the ugly ghoul. It had been a long time since her eyes were open in the sunlight. After all, the giant had always put her together during the night. The confused girl looked at Hassan Ali and asked "Who are you?" Hassan Ali told her who he was and how he had come to the fortress. He said that Mastaneh was waiting for him beyond the wall. "Who might you be and what brought you here?" Hassan Ali asked in return.

"I am Parvaneh," the girl said. "But before I explain anything else, we must find the ghoul's Bottle of Life and break it at once so that this cruel being will be banished forever! The horrible ghoul has a herd of sheep, which he pays close attention to. I think that his Bottle of Life is among them."

Hassan Ali looked around the large courtyard to find the herd of sheep. After spotting them, he carefully watched their behavior. Being a good shepherd, he noticed that one little lamb, thinner than the rest, had a slight limp. He caught the lamb and examined its weak leg. There, beneath the wool, he felt the Bottle of Life. With his knife, he cut out the bottle, and then carefully wrapped the lamb's leg with his handkerchief.

As soon as Hassan Ali raised the bottle to break it, the ugly ghoul rushed back with a thunderous roar, and threatened Hassan Ali and Parvaneh. He shouted, "Beware of my wrath and a harsh punishment!" Without fear or hesitation, Hassan Ali smashed the Bottle of Life on a rock, cracking it into two. The big ghoul became weaker and cried out, "Please, do one last thing before I die. Break my Bottle of Life one more time, so that I will not suffer." Parvaneh cried out to Hassan Ali, "Do not listen to him! If you break the Bottle of Life once more, the ghoul will come back to life and be even stronger!" Hassan Ali took the pieces of the broken bottle and buried them separately. The ghoul fell to the ground and lived no more.

Hassan Ali told Parvaneh, "We must go to Mastaneh, who is waiting on the other side of the wall." They ran to the wall and climbed over it. Mastaneh was there, sitting and worrying. They told her what had happened.

Parvaneh told Hassan Ali and Mastaneh the story of her life. "My father was a king in a faraway land. When he reached old age, he wanted me, his only child, to be crowned as queen. But, alas, my father suddenly died. His evil prime minister made a secret deal with the ghoul to kidnap and imprison me far away from the palace. The devious prime minister then took over the kingdom and sat on the throne as the high ruler. I wish that one day I can return to my land and reclaim the throne." Hassan Ali and Parvaneh were saddened by her story.

Then Mastaneh told Hassan Ali and Parvaneh how she had run away from her father's palace. Hassan Ali said, "The hand of fate has brought two princesses here together. There must be a reason for this. Let us free Parvaneh's land from the evil prime minister."

Mastaneh suggested, "Let us collect all of these rubies and go to the land of Parvaneh. We will give some of the jewels as a present to the prime minister so that we can enter the palace. Then, we will plan what to do next."

"My land is very far away. How can we get there?" asked Parvaneh. Hassan Ali said, "Many years ago, I saved the life of a young bird. A cruel hunter had drawn his bow, about to pierce the bird with his arrow. I felt sorry for the poor creature, and pushed the hunter's bow away. In gratitude, the bird plucked out a feather, and told me that if I was ever in need, to burn it. The young bird said that its mother was a big powerful bird, and the smell of the burning feather would bring her to my aid. We can get to Parvaneh's land by burning the feather and bring the big bird to help us."

They walked towards the river. "Wait here while I prepare for the journey," Hassan Ali told the two princesses. Then, he went back to his village and bought a horse for Parvaneh, which he paid for in rubies. He got food and water, and bid farewell to his friends and family. Hassan Ali returned to the riverbank and the waiting princesses.

Hassan Ali burned the feather and soon after, a giant bird appeared in the sky and landed nearby. The small bird, after so many years, had grown into a majestic and powerful creature. The bird heard the purpose of their journey and told them, "The way to the land of Parvaneh is treacherous and difficult. I know a safe shortcut that will take you there in a few days. It would be best if I fly above and show you the way as you ride and follow me." The three riders followed the flying bird. After a few days, they reached the land of Parvaneh.

Parvaneh remembered the city well, and found the house of a friend of her late father in which to stay. The friend had a trustworthy servant. Hassan Ali filled a large tray with rubies and gave it to the servant to carry. Hassan Ali and the servant went to the palace, while the princesses waited safely in the house. The bird flew to a nearby mountain where it could not be seen.

Soon Hassan Ali and his servant reached the palace gate. They showed the rubies to the guards, and Hassan Ali said, "This tray of rubies is an unworthy present for the highest ruler of the palace." The guards looked at the pile of rubies and smiled. Knowing how much the ruler loved jewels, they sent a messenger to tell him about the wealthy visitor and his servant. The ruler was delighted, and told the messenger to immediately bring them as guests into the palace.

Hassan Ali and his servant entered the castle. They walked down a long corridor with many fine carpets. They reached the high ruler and bowed down. Then, the servant put the tray filled with rubies at his feet. Hassan Ali told the ruler that he had a message from his father:

> *"My dear son, I am very proud of your success. I wish that you will come see me."*

The ruler stood up angrily and shouted, "My father passed away long ago!" Hassan Ali answered in a calm voice, "Indeed, your father has indeed passed from this world and is in the Other World, from where I come." The high ruler looked incredulously and asked, "How can this be? Give me a reason to believe you." Hassan Ali said, "Tomorrow, I will bring you a letter from your father with his own seal." Then, Hassan Ali and his servant bowed and left the palace.

When Hassan Ali returned to the two princesses, they discussed how to get a letter sealed by the ruler's late father. Parvaneh said, "My grandfather was a wise and good king. He had a prime minister that was also good and wise. When my grandfather died and my father took over the throne, the old prime minister served him well. But alas, the trusted minister also passed away. His greedy son, the current ruler, was not like his father. He became prime minister, and brought me to my sad fate. Since childhood, I have known the palace well, and I still remember all of the rooms. There is a room with a tiny window in which you can find the old seal of the ruler's father. We need to find a way to get this seal."

Hassan Ali thought that the giant bird may be of help. He took out another feather and burned it, and the giant bird immediately appeared. The bird suggested, "I have a friend, a small and daring dove, who can help. The dove can enter the room through the tiny window and bring us the seal. After we write and seal the letter, the dove can return the seal to its original place." So, the dove was called upon and provided this favor.

Parvaneh knew the handwriting of the old prime minister and was good at calligraphy. She wrote a letter in his handwriting saying:

"My brave son, pass through the fire and come see me."

Parvaneh then sealed the letter and the dove returned the seal.

The following day, Hassan Ali and the servant reached the gate of the palace with another tray full of rubies. The guards let them in to see the high ruler. As before, they bowed before the ruler and placed the jewels at his feet. Hassan Ali said, "I have brought a sealed letter from your father."

The high ruler opened the letter and read it. He asked Hassan Ali, "How can a person go through fire and reach the Other World?" Hassan Ali explained, "Order your servants to put a bed in the middle of the courtyard for you to sit on. Around the bed, have them make a fire. I will read a secret prayer and you will then be able to see your father." The high ruler said, "If you have lied to me, your punishment will be death!" Hassan Ali bowed his head and said, "May justice be our witness." So, the ruler's servants put a bed inside the courtyard for him to sit upon. They put mounds of cinder and wood around the bed, and lit a fire. After the fire started and the flames reached high into the sky, the giant bird flew into the middle of the thick smoke, and plucked out the greedy ruler with its claws. The bird took him to a place far away from the palace, where faithful soldiers of Parvaneh's late father were waiting. The soldiers put the evil ruler into prison.

Parvaneh returned to her palace, accompanied by the soldiers. She told her story to everyone in the palace. They were happy to see the lost princess back in her rightful place, and their hearts were filled with joy. Parvaneh sat on the throne and was crowned queen, according to her late father's wishes.

The giant bird brought Mastaneh back to her father's castle and Hassan Ali back to his village. Mastaneh's father was very happy to see his missing daughter. The princess told her father all about her adventures and asked him for forgiveness. Being a wise king, he said to Mastaneh, "Hassan Ali, the son of my prime minister, is a cowardly young man. He is not suitable for you. But Hassan Ali, the shepherd, is a brave and pure-hearted soul. It is time to bring Hassan Ali, the shepherd, to the palace, and I will anoint him as my trusted advisor."

Mastaneh smiled and coyly asked her father, "So, now I do not need to run away and marry Hassan Ali, the shepherd?" The king smiled happily, and arranged a beautiful wedding for the two young adventurers. Hassan Ali became a most trusted advisor. Mastaneh and her wise husband lived happily together for many years.

As for Parvaneh, she married a long lost friend that she had played with as a child in the palace while growing up, and also lived happily ever after. The two kingdoms of Parvaneh and Mastaneh lived in peace and harmony for many, many years.

11

The Little Salt Donkey

Once upon a day and once upon a time, under the purple dome of the sky, there was a mother donkey and her little baby donkey. Every day the donkey's owner took the mother donkey to work and came back at the end of the day. When she returned, the baby donkey was very happy to see her. He pranced, and he danced, and he brayed, and was so excited to see his mother again.

One day the little donkey asked his mother, "What do you do when you go to work every day?" The mother replied, "There is a salt lake very far from the city. There, the owner collects salt and loads it into my packsaddle. Then, he takes me to the market where he sells it all."

The little donkey asked, "What does salt look like?" The mother answered, "It is all white and made of tiny crystals that shine in the light. The salt surrounds the lake like the halo of the moon." "What does the lake look like?" asked the inquisitive little donkey. The mother answered, "It looks like a magical white place, where the water around the lake has dried, and white salt has remained. From far away, the surface of the lake looks like a mirror reflecting the light of the sky. But as you get closer, you can see that there is also water left in the middle of the lake. At times, you can see flamingos flying above with their pink reflections in the water."

The little donkey started to jump up and down, and kicked his hind legs back in excitement, and cried, "That sounds so beautiful! I want to see it, too!" The mother said, "You are too young and the load is too heavy. Wait until you are older and able to carry such a heavy load."

The next day, the little donkey woke up early and jumped up and down. He asked his mother, "Am I ready today? I want to bring salt! I want to bring salt!" And the mother answered, "No dear, you are not ready today." Day after day, the little donkey begged his mother, "Am I ready today? I want to bring salt! I want to bring salt!" And the mother would say, "Wait a little longer."

One morning, the mother thought, "Maybe it is a good idea to take my little donkey to the salt lake so that he can taste the hardship of work." She called her little donkey, and told him that he was ready to come to the salt lake with her. "Stay close behind me and do not stray away," she cautioned.

They went out of the house and all of the other donkeys stared at the little donkey and asked, "Where are you going?" The little donkey jumped up and down and said, "Salt! Salt! I am going with my mother to the salt lake to bring salt!" In fact, the little donkey excitedly jumped up and down all the way until they reached the salt lake.

The donkeys waited in the hot sun until the owner collected salt from the lake, and stood quietly as he loaded it onto their backs. The mother donkey asked the owner to put a tiny, tiny amount of salt in the pouches of the little donkey's packsaddle. From there, they walked to the market, where the owner unloaded all of the salt to sell.

The little donkey was very tired, and hungry, and thirsty. "When are we going home?" asked the tired little donkey. "When are we going home?" The mother donkey answered, "After all the salt has been sold." So they waited, and waited some more.

Finally, they headed back. On the way home, other donkeys saw how tired the little donkey was and asked him, "Where have you been?" The little donkey, with his head down, was exhausted, and hungry, and thirsty. He answered in a low, low voice, "Salt. I... went to... bring... s....salt." When they reached home, the little donkey ate oats, drank water, and fell fast asleep. After that day, he never asked his mother to bring salt again, until he was ready.

12

The Wheel of Fortune

Once upon a day and once upon a time, under the purple dome of the sky, there was a very unlucky man called Mehran. He failed at everything he tried. As time went by, he lost all hope and became sadder and sadder. One day, a wise man asked him, "Why are you so sad?" "I have very bad luck," moaned Mehran. The wise old man told him that he could change his luck and be successful if he left his home and travelled to a different place.

So, the unlucky Mehran packed the few things that he had, put them in a bundle along with some provisions, and started walking. He packed a canteen of water with some bread and onions, which were enough for one or two days. Mehran walked outside of the city, and was so deep in thought about his bad luck and difficult situation that he lost track of the days.

Soon, his provisions ran out and he had no food or water. Mehran felt very sad and thought to himself, "My luck has just gone from bad to worse." Suddenly, he heard soft chanting from far away. He ran to see where the voices were coming from and soon reached a small village. He went closer and closer until he got near enough to hear the familiar Friday evening prayers.

"Let us go, my beloved, to receive the bride,
And welcome the Day of Rest."

Mehran entered the place of worship and saw the congregation praying heartily. He soon joined in, but had a heavy heart and tearful eyes. Even though everything was so familiar, things looked so very different, but he couldn't quite put his finger on why he thought so. Everyone in the place of worship was very kind and hospitable. They asked him to stay with them to eat supper and to be their guest on the Day of Rest.

The unlucky Mehran began to worry, as he always did, and anxiously asked "Who are you and what is this place?" The hosts answered in a calm, soothing voice, "Sleep well and relax, and after the Day of Rest we will explain everything to you." Their kind and welcoming words calmed Mehran, and for the first time in many years, sadness left his heart and he fell into a deep sleep.

As soon as the Day of Rest ended, the hosts explained to Mehran, "We are fairies and would rather be hidden and out of sight. We only appear to those whom we choose, and only they can hear us. And now we have some questions for you. Why are you travelling alone? What brought you to this place?" Mehran told the fairies his sad, unlucky story and asked, "Dear fairies, could you help me change my fortune?"

The fairies invited Mehran to follow them into a big hall. There, he saw a huge wheel spinning around and around. The fairies said, "This is the Wheel of Fortune." Mehran saw that there were many priceless objects hanging off the wheel – deep red rubies, shiny green emeralds, pink diamonds, glittering pieces of gold and silver, and many works of exquisite miniature art.

Mehran asked, "What are all these beautiful things?" The fairies answered, "These are the fortunes of people. They are priceless, for they belong to one person, and one person alone." Now this made Mehran curious and he asked "Does everyone have a priceless fortune on this wheel?" The fairies answered, "Every person's luck is undoubtedly valuable."

The unlucky Mehran, asked, "Which one of these represents my fortune?" Expecting to see a priceless jewel, he closed his eyes. The fairies spun the wheel, and it went round and round until it finally stopped turning. Mehran opened his eyes to see what was on the Wheel of Fortune. The objects he saw were neither valuable nor the worthy art of a craftsman. They were worthless items: a piece of wood, a broken clay jar, and other ordinary things. Among them, he also saw an ugly, worn-out corroded piece of metal. The fairies pointed to the metal and told him, "This is your fortune."

Once again, sadness fell upon Mehran. He cried bitterly and asked, "Does this mean that I will be sad and a failure all of my life?" The fairies answered, "By no means! There is a way to change your corroded piece of metal into the most valuable diamond." Mehran asked, "In which way can I do so?"

The fairies explained, "In a nearby village, there lives a man called 'Kamanar, the Bloodthirsty'. He is called that because he hunts, and he is wild, and he is dirty, and everybody is afraid of him. The whole neighborhood left because they couldn't stand to be around such a disgusting and filthy man. He lives in a house with his wife and daughter. If you can help him change his ways and turn him into a well-behaved person, then your fortune will change and you will be one of the happiest people in the world."

Mehran went to Kamanar's village and inquired where he lived. The villagers looked at him in surprise and cautioned, "Kamanar is a wild and ill-behaved man. It is best to stay away from him." Nonetheless, Mehran found his house. He then found a place to hide nearby, and carefully noted Kamanar's comings and goings.

The area around Kamanar's house was horrible. There were mounds of bones and large hunks of raw meat. There were piles of dirt and filth. There was an intolerable smell of rotten dead animals. Mehran pinched his nose with his fingers, and stayed in his hiding place and watched. He saw that Kamanar got out of the house every morning, went to hunt, and came back every evening before the sun set, carrying the day's catch.

After a few days, Mehran started to clean up the place. Every day, after Kamanar had left, Mehran carried out bones and rotten meat, and buried them in a field outside of the neighborhood. He swept and cleaned all of the filth away. He continued doing this every day, little by little, until one day, all of the area around the house was nice and clean.

Now, in all of the days that Mehran hid watching the house, he had never seen Kamanar's wife or daughter. But one day, as soon as Kamanar left to go hunting, his wife and daughter walked out onto the front doorstep. They looked around and were very surprised to see such clean surroundings. Mehran cautiously crept out of his hiding place and began to talk to them, asking how they were.

They were very frightened to see a strange man near their house, and Kamanar's wife warned him anxiously, "Run, run away quickly, for if my husband, Kamanar, sees anybody around our house, he will become very angry and may harm you!" Mehran answered in a calm voice, "I know all about Kamanar and his ways. I know that he hunts and brings back animals, and is called bloodthirsty because he does so. And I know that others are afraid of him. But I am not afraid because I believe that in everyone's heart there is a light of kindness. I have taken an oath to help change your husband and turn him into a nice person. To do so, I need your help." Kamanar's wife and daughter, who had been left alone and forgotten, readily agreed to cooperate. They could not believe their good luck in having this stranger enter their lives.

From that day on, Mehran taught the wife and daughter how to clean the house, and how to take out all of the piled up garbage and bury it outside. He taught them how to cook tasty meals. He showed them how to wash and mend their clothes. Every day before sunset, Mehran left the house and spent the night in one of the abandoned houses nearby.

In due course, the house became clean and beautiful. Each room looked evermore immaculate and took on a nice, fresh smell. Mehran also emptied the pond in the yard, cleaned it, and refilled it with fresh water that he drew from the well.

One day before the Day of Rest, Mehran brought some sweet drinks and some sweet bread. He told the wife and daughter, "Make Kamanar the tastiest meal for supper. Pour a sweet drink into your best cup and lay the bread on your most beautiful plate. Let him drink and eat well so that he feels calm and relaxed." Mehran helped them go to the public bath-house in the village. After bathing, Kamanar's wife and daughter came out dressed in their best clothes. For the first time, Mehran noticed how beautiful the daughter looked, and sensed a sweet feeling in his heart.

Kamanar's wife and daughter returned home and prepared the table for supper. Kamanar came home after a long, hard day of hunting.

He was tired and filthy and grumpy. The wife boiled some water and brought soap. She took off his shoes and washed his feet. She spoke to him kindly and helped him wash up, and then brought him some clean clothes.

Kamanar looked up and saw that his wife cared for him. He looked at his daughter and saw that she was beautiful. The inviting smell of the well-prepared food brought back pleasant memories of the past. He remembered his childhood days when his mother cooked warm delicious soups. It had been such a long time since he had felt so good.

The family gathered around the table. They ate and drank and told stories. They spoke nicely in calm tones to one another. That night, Kamanar fell into a good, deep sleep. He had not slept like this in a long, long time. He slept till noon the day after, and for the first time in his life, felt like he was at peace with himself. The house was so nice and pleasant on that Day of Rest that he didn't even want to go hunting.

As the days went by, Kamanar became milder and milder. One day, as Kamanar was leaving his house, Mehran dared to show himself and greet him. Kamanar was very suspicious and didn't talk very much, but he was also not as angry as he had once been. In the days after, Mehran talked to Kamanar with respect and in a friendly tone. Soon, the villagers were surprised to see them walking and talking together, as though they had been lifelong friends.

Mehran suggested to Kamanar, "Instead of hunting every day, it may be a good idea to find a job in the village." Kamanar was tired of hunting, and agreed to leave his rough ways behind. With Mehran's help, he found a job in a shop working for an old shoemaker. Now that Kamanar was working, and had changed his ways, his neighbors returned back to their old neighborhood.

Kamanar's daughter, who had blossomed into a fine young lady, felt a deep love for Mehran, and Mehran had fallen in love with her. One day, he had the courage to ask for her hand in marriage. Kamanar and his wife happily agreed. The two were soon married and lived in a nearby house, happily ever after.

In the fairy village, Mehran's corroded metal on the Wheel of Fortune turned to a very beautiful rare and precious diamond, one of the most valuable jewels on the wheel.

13

The Caliph and the Clown

Once upon a day and once upon a time, under the purple dome of the sky, there was a jovial caliph who loved to eat fish. One day, his chefs prepared some delicious fish for him. While he was eating, a bone got stuck in his throat. His servants brought him water and many kinds of drinks to see if the bone could be loosened and made to go down his throat and relieve his pain. But nothing helped. The court doctors were summoned, and gave the poor caliph many different potions. Alas, no medicine could reduce his pain or dislodge the bone. The caliph was uncomfortable and sad.

The courtiers of the palace tried to make the caliph happy again and took him to a balcony high up, where he could see the city plaza and the bazaar. Many people were coming and going, buying and selling, and visiting one another. Among other things, the caliph could see a clown surrounded by a large crowd of people who were laughing.

The clown's acts made the caliph laugh so much that he couldn't stop. He laughed so hard that the bone jumped right out of his throat. After being in pain for so many days, he felt better and was happy once more. He ordered his courtiers to go and bring the clown to the palace.

The clown was indeed a very funny fellow, but he was always afraid of being told that he had done something wrong, or had made a mistake. When he saw the palace courtiers approaching, he quickly made his last few jokes, gathered his things, and ran away from the market stall.

The courtiers ran after him, but the fearful clown ran faster. One of the caliph's men was particularly swift, and caught the running clown by his elbow. Frightened, the clown said, "As God is my witness, I have done nothing wrong. Please, have mercy upon me!" He put on a funny, childlike, pouting face and begged, "In God's name, please let me go home!"

The courtiers said, "Dear clown, have no fear. We have not come here to arrest you. The caliph has invited you to his palace." The surprised clown stammered, "What? Why?" The courtiers answered, "The caliph had a bone stuck in his throat and when he saw your clown act, he began to laugh so hard that it finally came out. This is why he has invited you to his palace. He wants you to be the court clown." The clown calmed down a bit and followed the courtiers to the palace.

As they neared the palace, the clown began to worry again. He tried to remember all of his jokes and funny acts, especially those that made people laugh the loudest and the longest. He tried to rehearse in his mind how he would make the caliph laugh. Even though he was very nervous, he tried to calm himself.

The first week went fine. The clown put on many funny acts and told many funny jokes and the caliph laughed heartily. The caliph asked the clown to be the court jester and make him laugh every day.

After several months, the clown again began to worry. He had already told all of his jokes and had performed all of his funny acts. "The caliph will surely kick me out of the palace if I can't think of new funny things to do," he moaned.

After several days and nights of worry, he thought of an idea. "There are a lot of people serving the caliph," he thought to himself. "I can make jokes about all of his servants." So, the funny clown made jokes about all of the caliph's servants. He made jokes about the tall ones. He made jokes about the small ones. He made jokes about the bald ones. He even made jokes about the cooks, and the guards, and the stable boys, and made the caliph laugh every day.

Some of the servants liked the jokes made by the caliph's favorite clown and laughed and laughed. But others did not, especially the fat mean cook. One day, the cook brought lunch for the caliph and placed it on the table. The caliph angrily asked, "Why aren't there any apples?" The clown said, "The cook washed them, poured sugary syrup over them, and turned them over the fire until they became golden brown. Then he popped them into his mouth and ate them all up!" The clown mimicked the fat, mean cook gulping down all of the apples, and the caliph laughed at his silly antics. The cook nervously left and went back to the kitchen.

When the caliph finished eating, he began to worry. He told the clown, "I have twenty golden apples in my treasury room made by a master craftsman. I am very fond of these precious items, and am afraid that someone will steal them. Come with me to check that everything is fine." The caliph and his trusted clown hurriedly went to the treasury room. The caliph started to count the golden apples and found that some were missing! The caliph called his guards and told them to go and search the cook's quarters. Lo and behold, they found the precious apples hidden there in a chest! The greedy cook had stolen the key to the treasury room and had taken some of the golden apples. He confessed and was brought before the caliph. "Leave this place and never show your face here again!" decreed the caliph.

After this, the caliph decided that he should be more careful with his keys and keep them well-hidden. Now he trusted the clown even more than before. The caliph thought to himself, "I should pay more attention to this clown. His jokes may tell me what is happening around me."

One day, the caliph hid a key to an important room of the palace, and forgot where he had put it. He tried and tried to remember where it was, but couldn't recall its hiding place. He called the clown and said, "Stay by my side as I walk around the palace to search for my key." The caliph was so busy thinking about the lost key that he entered the bathhouse of his harem.

The clown was so stunned by what he saw that he didn't know what to do. He looked at the caliph shyly and said, "Your highness, there are openings here covered with wool. It is best that your humble servant leave." The caliph's eyes lit up and he cried in happiness to the clown, "Excellent, clown! Excellent! Now I remember where I put it!" The caliph ran out of the bathhouse towards the castle orchard, with the bewildered clown running after him. As soon as he left the harem, the clown heaved a deep sigh of relief. He thanked God that he was still alive, because in those days, no one but the caliph was allowed into the harem, on pain of death!

The clown did not understand why the caliph was so happy. But as soon as the caliph had reached the orchard, he went to a far wall, and took out his key from a hole that was covered with a fine cashmere woolen shawl.

Springtime came, and the happy caliph decided to go hunting and take the clown with him. As usual, the clown was afraid and thought worriedly, "This cannot go on for long. One day I will run out of clever things to say, and not have any more funny acts or jokes to tell. Then the caliph will banish me from the palace. Today, when the caliph is busy hunting, I will run away into the forest and disappear."

As they entered the hunting grounds, the clown remembered a poem and recited it under his breath:

> "Oh cricket, jump once,
> Oh cricket, jump twice,
> In the palm of my hand,
> You will jump thrice!"

A guard nearby heard the poem. He looked at the caliph and noticed a big black wasp jumping from his master's back, ready to sting his neck. The guard quickly caught the wasp and saved the caliph's life. The guard turned to the clown and said, "It was a black wasp, not a cricket!" The clown had hoped that on this hunting day he could run away into the forest and disappear. But now, he had an even higher position in the palace because he had unwittingly saved the caliph's life!

They came back from hunting and the caliph told the clown, "Dear clown, you have saved my gold, you have saved my key, and now you have saved my life. But the reason I like you the most is that it seems as if you never worry, and can always make me laugh." When the clown heard these words, he decided not to worry anymore and just be himself. He lived happily in the palace, and told many new jokes, and did many funny acts, and unknowingly protected the caliph for many, many years to come.

14

The Lazy Children

Once upon a day and once upon a time, under the purple dome of the sky, there was a family with three very lazy children. The parents did all of the work, while the children sat all day and did nothing but rest. None of them helped cook or clean. If a door was left open, no one would bother to close it. The parents complained to their children that they were very lazy and didn't move a finger to help, but the children did not care. So, the parents decided to teach them a lesson.

One autumn day, as the days became colder and colder, all of the doors and windows were open. The parents knew that if they weren't closed by the end of the day, the house would become very cold.

The father turned to the lazy eldest son and asked, "Can you close the door and all of the windows?" The son answered, "Why me? I am the eldest and my younger brother and sister should respect me." The father asked the lazy middle sister, but she said, "Why me? I closed the door last month. It's someone else's turn." When the youngest son was asked, he answered, "I have already done enough work today."

Unlike the other days, the parents sat down and didn't do anything. The children argued for some time. Eventually, they decided they would not talk, and that the first person to utter a word would have to get up and close the door and all of the windows.

They sat down and stayed quiet. The wind became stronger and the house became colder. The mother asked her children, "Could someone close the door and all of the windows?" The eldest brother grunted like this: "ah-ah, ah-ah". The middle sister cooed like this: "oo-oo, oo-oo". The youngest brother screeched like this: "ee-ah, ee-ah".

Just as the youngest was screeching "ee-ah, ee-ah", a little donkey came into the room and brayed loudly, "ee-ya, ee-ya". This startled the younger brother, who jumped up. He took the rope that was around the donkey's neck, led it outside, and closed the door. The little donkey seemed thirsty, so the young boy brought it some water to drink. After having its fill of water, the donkey playfully nuzzled its nose into the boy's chest. The boy laughed and thought that it would be fun to ride the donkey. As soon as he sat on its back, the little donkey started to run quickly, knowing just where it wanted to go.

They reached a house in the village and the donkey stopped and brayed. The owner of the house ran out. He was happy to see his lost donkey, and asked the boy how he knew where to come. The young boy told him how the donkey had entered his house, and how they eventually reached here.

The owner said, "This is my favorite donkey and it was stolen from me. As a reward, I will give you some money." The gentle animal again nuzzled up to the young boy and rubbed its neck against the boy's arm. The owner, seeing that the little donkey liked the boy, said, "If you want, you can work for me, and help clean the donkey, and feed it every day, and I will pay you for the job."

The youngest son came back home and told his family about the donkey's owner and his new job. He decided to never be lazy again, which made his parents very happy.

The older brother and sister, as lazy as ever, were still sitting and not talking. The windows were still ajar. A large gust of wind blew in and the room became very cold. The father turned to his two older children and asked, "Can one of you close the windows?" The lazy eldest son, still not wanting to talk, grunted like this: "ah-ah, ah-ah". The lazy middle sister, still not wanting to talk, cooed like this: "oo-oo, oo-oo".

Just as the sister said "oo-oo, oo-oo", a pigeon sat down on the window sill and cooed sadly, "roo-roo, roo-roo". The middle sister got up and saw that the poor bird's leg was hurt. She took the pigeon into the room and closed the window. "Poor thing!" she said as she looked at the suffering bird. "You look so hungry and thirsty." She gave it some water and bread crumbs, and bandaged its leg in a clean white cloth. Then she noticed that there was a note wrapped around the bird's other leg. She carefully removed the note and realized that it was a message for the ruler of the village.

The girl put on a warm sweater and some warm boots, and walked to the ruler's house. The ruler, who was waiting for the message to be delivered, was very happy to see the pigeon. Then he noticed that the bird had a wounded leg that had been bandaged, and realized that the girl had helped his pigeon. He said, "You were so caring and loving to my dear bird. If you wish, you can have a job caring for my pigeons. You can feed them and give them water every day, and I will pay you well."

The middle sister returned home and told her parents about the ruler and his pigeon. She decided that she would never be lazy again, which made her parents very happy.

The wind started to blow stronger. A window was still open, making the house colder. But the lazy eldest son was still sitting and didn't want to talk or move. The mother asked him, "The other window is still open. Can you close it?" The lazy son grunted, "ah-ah, ah-ah".

Just as the son grunted "ah-ah, ah-ah", a little monkey jumped on the window sill and cried, "ah-uh, ah-uh". The monkey came into the living room and jumped around. Then, it climbed right onto the eldest son's head! The boy shook the monkey off, and while doing so, noticed that the animal had a gold band around its neck. Looking more carefully, he saw that it was engraved with the name of a magician. The eldest son had heard of this magician, and decided to take the monkey back to its owner.

He closed the window and took the monkey to the marketplace. He asked the shopkeepers, "Do you know where the magician lives?" A shopkeeper answered, "If you go down this narrow alley, you will find a small house with a small door. That is where the magician lives." So, he took the monkey and walked down the narrow alley. He found the small house and knocked on the small door. The magician opened the door and was surprised to see his monkey. "My lost monkey!" he cried. "Now I can do my magic tricks again!"

He said to the boy, "My monkey is very precious to me. Because you have brought my dear monkey back to me, and did not steal the gold band around its neck, I know that you are trustworthy. If you like, you can be my apprentice, and I will teach you how to do magic tricks."

The eldest son came home and told his parents about the magician and his monkey. He decided that he would never be lazy again.

From that day on, the children were no longer lazy, which made their parents very, very happy. Because the doors and windows were closed in the autumn and the winter, the house stayed warm and cozy for many, many years.

15

Rose and Marigold

Once upon a day and once upon a time, under the purple dome of the sky, there lived a king who had a very beautiful and clever daughter. But the princess was very sad. Whenever her father said that he wished to see her happily married, the princess replied, "My dear father, you know why I am so sad."

One day, the king told the princess, "Among your many suitors, whoever can answer my riddle will be worthy of marrying you." The princess asked, "What is this riddle?" The king answered,

> *"What did Rose say to Marigold and what did Marigold say to Rose?"*

The princess immediately understood the meaning of the riddle and accepted her father's suggestion. She said, "I hope that a bold and noble man will be able to solve it."

The messengers of the king went to all the corners of the land and announced the riddle. Soon after, many young men, whose greatest wish was to marry the princess, came to the castle. Among them were those who thought that the riddle was a ploy for the princess to choose the best suitor by herself. Such suitors came dressed in expensive clothes, full of shining jewels and swooned:

> *"A rose with golden leaves and rubies asked a marigold full of diamonds and emeralds which one of us are worthy of the princess?"*

But soon, they realized that the princess wasn't interested in flowery sayings or jeweled attire.

Other hopeful suitors wrote poems about roses and marigolds and spring and ecstatic love, but the princess was still disappointed. The suitors soon lost hope as she left the reception hall with a regretful sigh.

There came a day, when a bold and wise shepherd thought to himself, "This riddle is not about money and wealth or poetry or beauty. It is about an adventurous journey." The shepherd went to the bathhouse, changed into his best clothes, and rode off to the palace. The castle guards were surprised to see such a simple suitor. They looked upon him with disdain, but remembered that the king had ordered to let in any suitor who reached the palace.

The shepherd had heard many stories of the princess's beauty, but was overwhelmed to see that she was even more beautiful than he had ever imagined. Yet, he could see deep sadness in her eyes. The bold shepherd asked, "Dear Princess, how much time do I have to solve this riddle?" The princess, finally hearing someone ask a sensible question, looked up hopefully and answered, "However long it takes."

The emboldened shepherd returned to his village and visited an old man, known for his great wisdom and vast experience. The wise old man carefully listened to the shepherd's story and advised,

"Only you can find your path. Wherever you go, look carefully and see all of the hidden signs that are around you. Before you take a step, look where you put your foot." The shepherd thanked him kindly and left.

The shepherd bid his family and friends farewell, and prepared supplies for his journey. The next morning, at the break of dawn, he started on his way. He passed through the beautiful fields of his village. Then, he reached a river and walked along its banks for many hours. Finally, he came to a point where the water diverted into a small stream. He followed this stream for a short time and saw that it poured into a big pond. Wild colorful flowers were growing around it. Their stems were so tangled that they had become a wall of flowery thorns, guarding a secluded area.

The exhausted shepherd sat down and opened his bundle of food. He ate meagerly and drank some water. As he was eating, he looked into the clear pond and saw a tiny golden fish suddenly appearing. He remembered the words of the wise old man.

The gold fish wriggled back and forth in the water and then dove back in, quickly disappearing into the depths below. The shepherd was surprised that he could no longer see the golden fish, since the water was very clear and it was possible to see to the very bottom of the pond.

The shepherd took a deep breath, jumped into the pond, and swam underneath to see where the golden fish had gone. There, beneath the water, he saw a cave-like passageway. At the other end, he could see the light of day. The shepherd returned to the surface, took a deep breath, dove back in, and swam into the cave. He swam for several minutes until he reached an opening at the far side of the cave and came up to the surface of the water, gasping for breath.

He came out of the water and looked around. Far away, hiding behind many trees, he saw a very high wall. The stones of the wall were grey and black. The shepherd felt an unexplained sadness as he looked upon it. He decided to find a way to get behind the wall and discover the secret of the sadness that fell upon him. He walked closer and closer to the wall.

The sun was slowly setting, and in the light of the dusk, the shepherd saw a large tree with thick, intertwined branches. He decided to spend the night on top of the tree. He climbed up and found a good branch on which to rest. From there, through the branches and leaves, he looked upon the dark wall. Behind it there was a strange house. Its doors and windows were much larger than ordinary, and the house looked dark and gloomy.

In another branch of the tree, there was a nest with a few baby birds waiting restlessly for the return of their mother. The shepherd suddenly saw that a big snake was creeping towards the nest, ready to attack and swallow the poor little birds. The bold shepherd swiftly caught the snake's neck with his bare hands, killed it, and flicked it away from the nest.

Soon after, a huge bird circled overhead, swooped down, and landed in the nest. The magnificent bird looked at the shepherd and exclaimed in joy, "You have saved my children! I owe you their lives!" The bird plucked out one of its feathers and gave it to the shepherd. "Take this feather and whenever you need my help, burn it. From the smell, I will know where you are, and come to your aid. But pray tell, what brings you to this dangerous land?"

The shepherd told the bird about his adventures and asked, "Who lives behind this dark wall inside of the strange house?" The bird answered, "A wicked and cruel ghoul lives there. Beware, for he often captures innocent people and imprisons them inside of his house!"

When the sun had already set and the night was approaching, a huge and ugly ghoul entered the gate and came into the yard. He sniffed into the air and growled,

> *"With what right, I shout,*
> *Is a human smell about?"*

Then, the ugly ghoul looked around and entered the house. The bird whispered into the shepherd's ear, "Every day, early in the morning, the ghoul leaves his house and after the sun sets, he returns."

The next morning, after the ghoul left, the shepherd asked the bird to take him behind the dark wall. The shepherd climbed onto the bird's back, and they flew over the wall into the ghoul's courtyard. The shepherd got off, looked around, and saw a half-opened window. He climbed through and entered the huge house.

He checked out each room until he heard a moaning voice coming from behind one of the doors. The shepherd opened the door and saw many people imprisoned inside several cages, which saddened him greatly.

Inside one of the cages, there was a thin, beautiful girl, who looked remarkably similar to the princess. She said to the shepherd, "If you have come to rescue us, before doing anything else, find the ghoul's Bottle of Life, and break it. Only after you have done this, come back and free us." One of the other prisoners added, "The ghoul's Bottle of Life is not inside the house. It is hidden somewhere in the yard."

Without fear, the shepherd quickly ran outside. He saw a little bird singing beautifully, and flitting among the trees. The shepherd noticed that one tree had one green branch among many dry, brown branches. Again, he remembered the words of the old wise man.

He climbed up the tree and examined the green branch carefully and discovered a hidden crack. The shepherd kicked the branch and broke it. Lo and behold, the Bottle of Life was hidden inside! He took it and quickly scrambled down the tree.

Soon after, the ghoul came rushing back, snorting like thunder and lightning. First, he tried to scare the shepherd but when he saw that the shepherd was not afraid, he tried to fool him. But the shepherd could not be fooled, either. The shepherd did not waste a minute. He bashed the Bottle of Life with one sharp hit on a hard stone, breaking a part of it off.

The ghoul suddenly became weak and fell on the ground with a heavy thud. He said in a weak, tiny voice, "I am almost gone. Take my broken Bottle of Life and hit it one more time so that it will shatter completely and I will no longer suffer." But the shepherd knew by the wisdom of ages that hitting the Bottle of Life twice would bring the ghoul back to life and make him even stronger. The shepherd buried each piece of the broken bottle under the soil in different corners of the yard.

Then, the shepherd rushed into the ghoul's house and asked the prisoners, "Where are the keys to your cages?" With their guidance, he found the keys and freed everyone. All of the prisoners crowded around him in gratitude and asked, "Why did you endanger your own life to free us? How can we repay your kindness?"

The shepherd told them the story of his adventures and asked, "Could you help me solve the king's riddle?"

"What did Rose say to Marigold and what did Marigold say to Rose?"

The thin, beautiful girl spoke up:

"The riddle is about the story of my life. Many years ago, my sister and I were two princesses, happy, and jovial, and carefree. My elder sister's name is Rose and I am Marigold. Rose always looked after me. One day, my sister and I went outside to play. I carelessly wandered outside of the castle grounds. The cruel ghoul was waiting for such a moment. He suddenly pounced upon me and grabbed me with his ugly claws. The guards of the castle could not release me from the claws of the ghoul but were successful in saving my sister.

As I was carried off, Rose cried out,

'I will free you from the cruel ghoul!'

And I, Marigold, answered with tears in my eyes,

'I hopefully look forward to that day.'"

Marigold continued. "That fateful day, the ghoul screeched to the soldiers in a piercing voice that the king must give him the throne if he wants his daughter back. But my father, the king, was not ready to let the lives of all of his people fall into such ruin, even if it meant that he could not save his own beloved daughter."

The shepherd took out the magic feather of the bird and burned it. The giant bird quickly landed in the ghoul's courtyard. The shepherd said, "First, take Marigold and return her to the palace and her waiting family. Then, come back here and take the other prisoners." The great bird did so. The last one to return safely to his village was the shepherd himself.

Marigold was reunited with her long lost family, and all were very excited to see her. Happiest of all was her sister Rose. Marigold told them about the courageous and noble shepherd who had freed her and all of the prisoners.

The shepherd felt relieved, and was glad that everyone had reached home safely. He went to the bathhouse and put on his best clothes. Now knowing the answer to the riddle, he rode off to the castle to win Rose's hand in marriage.

Rose, happier than ever and more beautiful than any flower, was waiting at the gate to see him. The king arranged a beautiful wedding and they lived happily ever after.

16

The Mother-in-Law and the Snake

Once upon a day and once upon a time, under the purple dome of the sky, there was a man called Ramin who was very unlucky. Whatever business he tried failed miserably, and his life was full of one disappointment after another. Ramin never had enough money to pay for all of the family expenses. To make matters worse, even though his wife was very sweet, his mother-in-law made his life bitter and his load heavier. She constantly nagged and complained, and told him how inept and useless he was.

One day, Ramin went to open his heart to an old wise man. Experienced in the ways of the world, the old man advised him to go and travel to another place. The old man explained, "According to the wisdom of old times, if you change where you live, your luck will surely change for the better."

So Ramin travelled to another city. He saw the caliph's messengers standing in the public square, delivering an announcement:

> *"There is a big nasty snake in the palace. If there is any man who is courageous enough to come and take the snake away, the caliph will reward him richly."*

Ramin thought to himself, "If I can trap the snake and take it out of the palace, maybe my luck will change." Without hesitating, he boldly stepped forward and said to the messengers, "Take me to the palace. I can catch the snake!" The messengers, seeing that nobody else stepped forward, gladly took him to the palace.

A sudden fear befell Ramin. After all, he did not have any experience with snakes. But he remembered that as a young boy, his mother told him to think before doing anything. He told the courtiers of the palace, "I will trap the snake and rid it from the palace forever. But in order to do so, I need a few days to observe how it behaves."

Ramin went to the orchard around the palace and looked at every nook and cranny. He found a suitable place, high up, where he could see the snake. He watched carefully, and saw where the snake came from and where it went. He saw what the snake ate and where it rested. He thought to himself, "If I can get a big trap with some bait, I can deceive the snake and catch it easily."

The next day, Ramin told the courtiers, "In order to catch the snake, I need a big trap." The courtiers brought a master craftsman to the palace, and Ramin explained how the trap should be built. The craftsman made the trap exactly as ordered.

Then Ramin told the servants, "Bring me some bait that is suitable for catching the snake." They did so, and Ramin put the trap with the bait in a corner of the garden where the snake liked to rest. Ramin sat down and waited patiently for a long time. As planned, the snake went to rest in its favorite spot. It smelled the delicious bait, went inside of the device to eat, and was trapped!

The caliph and all the people in the palace were very happy to hear that the big, nasty snake had been caught. The courtiers told Ramin,

"The caliph will reward you when you take this awful snake far away from the palace, and rid it from here for good."

Ramin asked for a cart and put the trap with the snake on it, tying it tightly. Then he set out to the fields outside of the city. He searched for a suitable place in which to throw the nasty creature. After many hours of riding, he reached a village and asked the villagers, "Where is a good place to get rid of this snake?"

The villagers said, "Outside of the village, there is an abandoned house with a dry well in the backyard. It is full of annoying mice that destroy everything. If you throw the snake into the well, you will get rid of the snake, and we will get rid of the mice." Ramin found the abandoned house and threw the snake into the dry well.

Ramin returned to the palace and was bestowed with all of the promised riches. The caliph and his servants were very relieved and happy. Even the high courtiers bowed to him and were grateful. Ramin was very happy, and proud of what he had done. He thought to himself, "My luck has finally changed for the better. At last, my mother-in-law will know my true worth."

Now that he was very wealthy, Ramin bought a big beautiful house in one of the best areas of the city, and brought his family to join him. He told them the story of how he had rid the caliph's palace of the snake.

Ramin's mother-in-law, who had never valued him, told him that she did not believe his story. He replied, "But even the caliph knows who I am!" His mother-in-law thought that he had simply made up the story, and continued to nag him. She even implied that he had stolen all that he had. Ramin was so fed up with her constant nagging that he told her, "Come! I will show you the well where I trapped the nasty snake."

Ramin got into a carriage with his mother-in-law, and they rode together to the well. When they got there, the mother-in-law looked into the well and complained that it was empty. Ramin said, "Look more carefully, for surely the snake is still there." As she bent down to look into the well to take a closer look, one of the stones suddenly loosened and she fell inside.

The snake was now used to this place, and was always well-fed with many delicious mice to eat. He was taking a nice nap at the bottom of the well when the mother-in-law suddenly crashed down on top of him and woke him up! She shouted, and screamed, and nagged so much that the snake couldn't stand it any longer. It summoned all of its energy, jumped out of the well, and found its way all the way back to the palace.

Meanwhile, Ramin found a rope and helped his mother-in-law get out of the well. They rode the carriage back home. When they reached there, the palace guards were waiting for him and said, "The caliph is very angry at you. The snake has come back. You promised that you would rid the palace of the snake forever, but you have not kept your word. Get the snake out for good or the caliph will punish you severely!"

Once again, fear and trepidation entered Ramin's heart. He said to himself, "Why have I always been so unlucky?" Then, a clever idea came to his mind. He thought, "If the snake ran away from my nagging mother-in-law from inside the well, I can take her to the palace and the snake will run away from her there as well."

Ramin called over the guards, and said, "Take me and my dear mother-in-law to the palace immediately." As soon as the mother-in-law entered the palace, the snake heard her nagging voice. It jumped up in great fear, and slithered all the way back to the dry well of the abandoned house.

The caliph, seeing the mother-in-law for the first time, thought that she was a woman of great courage and valor to have managed to scare off such a nasty snake. He instantly fell in love with her, and she lovingly gave her heart to him in return. He pronounced her as his queen, but she couldn't nag very much in the palace or the caliph would simply leave and go to his other wives.

From that day on, Ramin and his family lived a quiet and restful life. The snake never came back to the palace, and the villagers never suffered from mice again.

17

The Singing Doll

Once upon a day and once upon a time, under the purple dome of the sky, there was a very beautiful girl called Lobatak who sang sweetly. Lobatak and her mother lived in a village by the river. Every day, her mother went to the river and worked very hard washing clothes for a living. She soaped the clothes, beat them, and rinsed them until they were fresh and clean. Then she wrung them, dried them in the sun, and brought them back to their owners. Lobatak helped in the house while her mother was away.

One day, when Lobatak was helping with the household chores and singing sweetly, an evil witch passed by and heard her voice. She looked through the window and saw the beautiful girl. The witch, becoming more jealous with every note that Lobatak sang, thought to herself, "I should have a beautiful daughter like this so that I can turn her into a vicious witch!"

The witch entered the house, and stood in front of the young girl. Lobatak immediately stopped singing and asked in a frightened voice, "Who are you?"

The witch answered sweetly, "I am a fairy and if you come with me, I can make your voice more beautiful."

But Lobatak was clever and not easily deceived by such a cunning witch and replied, "My voice is beautiful enough, thank you."

"If you come with me, I can make your face more beautiful," said the witch.

"My face is beautiful enough, thank you," Lobatak replied.

"If you come with me, you will live in a palace with many riches," the witch continued.

Lobatak said, "I already live in my own palace. Even though we are not rich, we are rich in love and that is what counts. I love my family and will never leave my home, thank you."

Trying to entice Lobatak for one last time, the witch said, "If you come with me, you can become the most magical fairy in the land and learn all of my magic tricks!"

Lobatak asked, "Good magic or bad magic?"

With a sly and crooked smile on her face, the witch answered, "Magic that will make people do whatever you want."

Clever Lobatak replied, "Then that is bad magic! Go away and never come back to our house again!"

The witch got very angry and began to huff and puff. Steam came out of the top of her head. She screamed, "You nasty girl! I will turn you into a lifeless ugly doll with nothing but dirty clothes!"

The witch twirled around and said some incantations. Beautiful Lobatak turned into a lifeless ugly doll with dirty clothes.

When Lobatak's mother came back from a hard day of washing at the riverbank, she called out to her beautiful daughter, but no one was in the house. She strained to see if she could hear her beautiful daughter's voice, but she could not hear anything. Distraught, she ran to the neighbors and cried out, "Has anyone seen my beautiful daughter or heard her beautiful voice?" But no one had, and there was no sign of her. It was as if she had vanished into thin air. The poor mother cried and cried, and did not know how she could go on without her beautiful Lobatak.

The next morning, with a heavy heart, Lobatak's mother went out to wash clothes at the river. As soon as the mother had left the house, Lobatak turned back into a live girl, cleaning the house and cooking while singing. But when her mother returned home, Lobatak would again become a lifeless doll. The mother saw that the rooms were clean and in order. She sniffed and smelled the lovely fragrance of cooked food, and thinking that her daughter was there, became happy. She called out to Lobatak hoping to eat supper together, but there was no reply. Again, she ran to the neighbors and asked if anyone had seen her dear daughter. One of the neighbors said, "Today, I heard Lobatak's beautiful voice. She is not far from home."

Many days went by like this, until one day the prince of the land passed by along the river, accompanied by his soldiers and horsemen. As they neared the village, the prince heard the sweet voice of Lobatak, which was more beautiful than any voice he had ever heard. He told his soldiers to search the houses of the village and find the girl who sang so sweetly.

The prince's soldiers followed the sweet voice of Lobatak. As soon as the prince's men came closer to the house, the magic spell of the witch became stronger, and the girl turned back into a lifeless doll that could not sing.

The soldiers returned to the prince and said, "It is very strange. We hear a beautiful voice coming from a house in the village. But as soon as we get close to it, the singing stops and there is complete silence. It even seems as if there is nobody inside of the house at all." No one in the prince's company could explain this mystery.

The prince had fallen in love with this girl who had such a beautiful voice. The disappointed prince went back to his castle with his men. But as the days passed, the thought of the heavenly voice became stronger and stronger in the prince's mind. He could think of nothing else. The prince vowed to solve this puzzle, and find the girl who sings so sweetly.

The prince thought to himself, "Perhaps the girl was afraid of my soldiers and that is why she stopped singing." So, he disguised himself as a poor man and returned to her village alone. He came towards the house and heard her sweet songs, but even with worn-out clothes, as soon as he got closer, the singing stopped.

The prince was very determined, and he went back again and again to find the singing girl. His longing for her became deeper and deeper. Unbeknownst to the prince, each time he visited the village, the doll became more and more beautiful, and her clothes became cleaner and more colorful.

The king saw that his son had become sorrowful, and was always deep in thought. He asked the prince why he was so sad. The prince told him the story of the singing girl. The king asked for the wisest man in the land to come to the palace and help solve the mystery.

The wisest man in the land came to the palace and heard the story. He told the king, "There is a spell cast by a wicked witch in this village. The spell can be broken only by love." The prince was happy to hear that the spell could be broken and asked how it could be done.

The old wise man turned to the prince and answered, "Ask the gardener of the palace to bring you the most beautiful fragrant rose in the garden. Take the flower and go close to the house of the singing girl so that she can smell it. The mixture of the love in your heart with the rose's beautiful fragrance will break the witch's spell. But, be careful of the wicked witch. She may try to deceive you and pretend to be the singing girl. If you give her the rose, the evil witch will put you under a spell and you will never return!"

The gardener of the palace picked the most beautiful and fragrant rose in the garden and gave it to the prince. He took the rose, and rode to the village in his golden carriage, accompanied by his trusty horsemen. As soon as the prince entered the village, the witch turned herself into a beautiful girl, pretending to be the one waiting for him. The prince felt a sudden fear in his heart, and ordered the driver of the carriage to avoid her and continue riding speedily to Lobatak's house.

Soon after, the carriage reached Lobatak's house. The prince opened the door of the carriage, and the smell of the rose reached the house. Lobatak continued singing, even though there was someone close by. She smelled the beautiful fragrance and followed it outside of the house to the carriage, as if in a trance. When she saw the prince, she instantly fell in love with him. Seeing Lobatak's great beauty, the prince fell even more deeply in love with her. He stepped out of the carriage and handed her the rose. The evil spell was broken, and the witch's magic turned to purple dust, which rose in the late afternoon sky and disappeared among the orange clouds.

The sun had just set and Lobatak's mother came home after a tiring day of work. She was so happy to see her lost daughter. Running to her, she hugged and kissed her a thousand times. Then, she looked around and was surprised to see a golden carriage with the prince and all of his men.

Suddenly, the wicked witch appeared once more. Shrieking and shouting, she spun around, and recited evil incantations to turn everyone into lifeless dolls. But the love in the air and the fragrance of the flower reflected the evil magic towards the witch, and she, herself, turned into a lifeless doll.

Lobatak and her mother went back to the palace with the prince and his men. The young couple were married and lived happily ever after. As for the witch, she could only come to life when all of the donkeys of the village brayed together in a choir under a blue moon.

18

The Rich Father and His Sons

Once upon a day and once upon a time, under the purple dome of the sky, there was a father who was very rich. He had a number of sons, and they all lived comfortably in a lovely big house that looked like a castle. The house had many rooms and a courtyard full of beautiful trees and flowers. There was one room in the house that the sons disliked because it had a wall that was crooked and ugly. The rich father used this room to work and study.

The rich man encouraged his sons to work hard so that they would know the value of money, and see how difficult it was to earn a good living. But his sons were not interested in working hard. All they did was spend money foolishly and waste time enjoying life.

The father became very old, and called all of his sons to hear his last words. He said, "My dear sons, I want to divide my riches equally among you. My only request is that this house never be sold, and that you will not change anything within its walls. But, if you ever reach a point in your lives where you are filled with sadness, and all your happiness and hope are lost, then you can break the crooked wall in my office and rebuild it according to your taste."

After the rich man passed away, each son inherited a very large sum of money. The sons were so wealthy that they thought they would never need to work again. They threw lavish parties, traveled to far ends of the earth, and enjoyed all of the pleasures of life.

The sons did not notice that little by little they had spent all their money. After some time, there was none left. For the first time in their lives, they tasted hardship. The brothers had to work hard for a living and earn money. But they had never worked before, and soon became sad and hopeless.

The brothers began to cry. "We should have saved more money," wailed the youngest. "We spent all of our wealth foolishly," chimed in the eldest, sadly. "We should have listened to our father," moaned another.

Now, in their hour of sadness and without hope, they remembered their father's last words. The brothers decided to break the crooked wall that they had hated so much. Carrying pickaxes and sledgehammers, they gathered in their late father's office, and began to break down the wall. "Finally, we are getting rid of this ugly thing," said the eldest brother, with the final blow. The crooked wall crumbled down into a heap of rubble.

To their great surprise, they found another room hidden behind. It was full of many big chests, which they began to open. Lo and behold, the chests were laden with hidden treasures, full of gold coins and valuable jewels. The brothers saw a little chest near the back wall, smaller than all of the others. They opened it and found the biggest and most beautiful jewel of all, hidden inside.

Above it, there hung a parchment inside an inlaid frame, with two proverbs written in their father's handwriting:

"Outer appearance is deceitful."
"Learn the wisdom of gathering from the ants."

The sons had learned their lesson. From then on, they worked hard and enjoyed life. When they had children of their own, each son made a hidden treasure room covered by a crooked wall.

19

The Peri and Firuz

Once upon a day and once upon a time, under the purple dome of the sky, there was a young man called Firuz who was very poor and unlucky. No matter what Firuz did, it always ended in failure.

One day, the king's messengers announced that the prince was very ill and that anyone who could come and cure him would be rewarded handsomely. Firuz thought to himself, "If I go to the palace and succeed in curing the prince, I will become a very rich man."

He packed his bags and travelled several days to reach the palace. When he got there, he told the guards at the gate, "I can cure the prince, but I need to be alone with him in a quiet room away from everyone."

The guards took Firuz's message to the king. The king was worried because no one else had come to the palace to try to cure the prince. He ordered his courtiers to take his son to a suitable room and let Firuz try his luck. Several guards were posted near the door to make sure that no one else entered. Once in the room, alone with the sick prince, Firuz knelt and prayed to God for his luck to be changed, and that he would succeed in curing the prince.

After some time, a peri magically entered the room through a tiny window and said to Firuz, "I heard you praying. I can help you, but have two conditions. First, you may see how I cure the prince, but you must promise to never try anything like this when you are alone because you lack the proper skills. Second, you must promise that when you become rich, you will help all who are in need." Firuz promised the peri that he would do what was asked.

The peri pulled out a small case from under his arm and opened it. He took out some salve and smeared it on the neck of the prince. The prince instantly fell into a deep sleep. Then, the peri took out his knife and carefully cut open the skin on the prince's neck. The sick prince was in such a deep sleep that he did not feel the peri cutting him. The peri bent over the prince and took out a large dark lump from the prince's throat. Afterwards, he brought out another salve from his case, and dabbed it on the cut. The wound magically closed, and the prince's neck looked as if it had never been touched.

The peri showed the dark lump to the astonished Firuz and explained, "This is what was preventing the prince from breathing and eating properly, and why he was so sick. Tell the king that the prince will get better now. The prince must completely rest and eat soft foods until he regains his strength." The peri put his knife and all of his salves back into the case, and while leaving, turned to Firuz and reminded him of his promises.

After the peri left, the prince woke up. He put his hand on his neck. He was surprised that he was able to take deep breaths, and felt very happy that he was now cured. Firuz opened the door and announced to the guards, "The prince is now cured. Take me to the king."

Firuz told the king, "Your son's health has been restored. He will feel better as the days go on. Make sure that he rests and eats soft foods until he regains his strength." After a few weeks, the prince became healthy and strong.

Now that the prince had fully recovered, the king rewarded Firuz handsomely. Firuz became one of the richest men in the land and married the daughter of a nobleman. Alas, soon after, Firuz forgot about his promises to the peri and did not help those in need.

One day, Firuz heard that a princess in a faraway land was ill, and that her father had announced that anyone that could cure her would be rewarded richly. Hoping to become even richer, Firuz traveled there and told the guards, "I can cure the princess but I need to be alone with her in a quiet room away from everyone."

The king of this land was known to be very stern and warned Firuz, "If you fail to cure my daughter, you will be put to death! But if you cure her, you will receive great wealth and fine, precious jewels."

Firuz sat in a room near the princess's bed, without anyone else attending. He had brought a small case that looked the same as the one that the peri had carried, and with similar items inside. He examined the princess's throat, hoping to cut out a dark lump. However, he soon realized that her situation was very different from what he had seen before. He could feel no lump and did not know how to use the knife.

Time was passing, and Firuz, afraid of facing the king, became more and more anxious. As he was trying to remember all of the things that the peri had done, he realized that he had not kept any of his promises. Firuz began to cry, and prayed to God for forgiveness. At that moment, the peri magically appeared in the room. Firuz looked up and tearfully told him, "Forgive me, for I have not kept my promises to you." The peri answered, "Many a time, greed and jealousy make a man lose his way. If you break your promises once more, I will never come to help you again."

The peri checked the princess and cured her and went away. The king rewarded Firuz handsomely with money and jewels. As soon as Firuz left the palace, he saw a beggar, but now, he readily gave the poor man some money.

Firuz returned home and was thankful to have such a good family, and live in such a beautiful and comfortable house. From that day on, he helped the poor and helpless, and became known as a generous man. He never again pretended to be what he was not, and was forevermore happy with his lot.

20

The Jeweler and the Apprentice

Once upon a day and once upon a time, under the purple dome of the sky, there was a skillful jeweler who knew how to make the most beautiful jewels out of the hardest raw stones. Most jewelers would not dare to cut such hard rocks and would throw them away, judging them to be worthless. But, this jeweler was such a master that he could turn even the roughest stones into extremely rare pieces of jewelry.

One day, a child came to his shop, begging for bread. The jeweler told him, "Rather than beg, come clean and tidy my place and I will pay you for your work." So, the child-beggar earned his keep and no longer needed to beg for a living. The jeweler saw that the boy was trustworthy and talented, and decided to teach him his secrets of making jewels. As the years went by, the boy grew, and became a great talent himself, mastering the trade as well as his teacher.

One day, the young man told his master, "This city isn't big enough for two jewelers that make similar jewels and attract the same customers. I will move to another city and start my trade there." So, the young man thanked the jeweler for all that he had done for him, and went to a faraway city to start his own business.

After a number of years, the old jeweler suffered a chain of bad luck. Fewer and fewer customers came to his store. Those who did, bought fewer items, or worse, didn't pay the jeweler any of the money that they owed.

Eventually, the poor jeweler went broke and lost his business. With a heavy heart, he closed his shop. He didn't know where to go or whom to ask for help. Then he remembered his young apprentice in the faraway city, and decided to travel there.

The old jeweler packed his tools and started on his journey. After a long and arduous trip, he eventually reached the city where the young jeweler lived. He asked many people where he could find the young jeweler. All the people seemed to know of him, and directed the old man to the young jeweler's house. The old man finally made his way to an opulent and magnificent castle. He was happy at heart to see that his young apprentice, whom he loved as a son, had succeeded so well. A number of guards were standing at the gate of the house, and saw the old man coming towards them.

Tired from his long journey, and heartbroken from his string of bad luck, the old jeweler looked rumpled with dusty, creased clothes. As he approached the mansion, the guards looked at him suspiciously and asked gruffly, "What do you want, old man? Who are you?" The jeweler told the guards his name, and asked to see the master of the house. The guards went in, and after some time, came out and apologized, "The master is very busy at the moment and is not able to see you now."

Broken-hearted and disappointed, the old jeweler went to find cheap lodging with the little money that he had. Tired in body and soul, he found an inn to spend the night, and bought some bread and an onion to eat. Early the next morning, he rose and went to the courtyard to wash his face. A young boy came and asked, "Kind Sir, can you help me?" The boy took out a stone and said, "Can you buy this stone from me? No other jeweler is ready to pay a penny for it."

The old jeweler looked at the stone carefully and realized its worth. He understood why many jewelers wouldn't dare touch such a thing. Its outer edges were ragged, almost as ragged as his own clothes. One had to look closely at it from all angles in order to see its inner beauty. The thought came to him that he was still a skilled craftsman, even though he had lost everything. He said to himself, "I can turn this stone into one of the most beautiful pieces of jewelry. And then, I will not need help from anyone."

With the little money he had left, he bought the raw stone from the young boy. Renewed with hope, he feverishly began working on it. Being such a skilled jeweler, the old man soon turned it into a magnificently cut jewel.

The old jeweler went to the bazaar to find a customer for his precious jewel. He had barely reached the market when a rich, well-dressed man approached him and said, "Good day, Sir. I was told by someone who once knew you that you are a master craftsman. It is said that each one of your jewels is a beautiful work of art and a rare masterpiece. I wish that I could buy one of your jewels." The jeweler took out his newly made piece and showed it to the gentleman. The rich man looked over the jewel, admired it greatly, and bought it at a hefty price.

The jeweler couldn't believe his good fortune. He bought some fine clothes, had a nice haircut, went to the public bathhouse, and ate well. A wave of calmness rippled through his body. He decided to go back to his city.

As he started to arrange his trip home, another well-dressed man approached and politely said, "Your eminent craftsman, my master has sent me to take you to his house." The surprised jeweler asked, "Who is your master?" The man answered, "Your loyal apprentice who owes you everything." Tears welled in the old jeweler's eyes as he realized that his apprentice, the young jeweler, had arranged it all – the young boy, the rich customer who bought the jewel, and this polite man.

Soon after, the young jeweler stepped out of a nearby carriage and kissed the old man's hand. He said, "Forgive me, master. After a lifetime of what you have done for me, I could not bear to see you as a person in need." They wiped their tears and entered the carriage. Then, they rode to the young jeweler's house, where a lavish party had been arranged.

The old jeweler went back to his city and opened up his business again. He regained his wealth, and helped many other people throughout the years.

21

The Two Brothers

Once upon a day and once upon a time, under the purple dome of the sky, there were two brothers who worked on a farm. They both worked very hard to provide for their families, especially at harvest time when there was much work to be done. They gathered the sheaves of wheat from the fields and stacked them into big piles. They separated the chaff from the grains with pitchforks. At the end of the day, the brothers put the grains of wheat into large gunnysacks. Then they bound the sacks tightly with string. Each brother filled as many sacks as he could.

Every day before sunset, the brothers divided the gunnysacks equally between them, and each brother carried his share back to his own storehouse. Little by little, their storehouses started to fill up.

One night, just as the younger brother was ready to go to bed, he thought to himself, "My older brother has more children with more expenses. He needs more wheat than I do." So, as midnight approached, he carried a number of sacks from his storehouse, and put it into the storehouse of his older brother.

The same night, the older brother couldn't sleep until after midnight. He tossed and turned and thought, "My younger brother has not yet finished his house and is not as well-established as I am. He needs more wheat than I do." So, he carried a number of sacks of wheat from his storehouse, and put it into the storehouse of his younger brother. This went on for many days.

In a nearby forest, lived a family of fairies. They watched the brothers, and noticed how kind they were to one another, and how considerate they were of each other's needs. The fairies decided to help the two brothers.

After the harvest season, the two brothers worked hard plowing their lands. In the middle of the night, the fairies came out and plowed the soil even deeper. They turned the ground over, and replenished it with the best type of soil from the far corners of the forest.

In the planting season, the two brothers selected some seeds, and put them aside in gunnysacks for planting the next day. In the middle of the night, the fairies brought the best seeds from faraway lands, and mixed them with the other seeds in the sacks.

In the dry season, the brothers watered the wheat every day. In the middle of the night, the fairies brought special fairy water, and dripped one little drop at the roots of each sprout so that the stalks would grow taller and stronger.

In the harvest season, the farm produced more wheat than ever. The land was blessed for many years, and there was enough rain and plenty of good rich soil for the wheat to grow.

The fairies made a monument in honor of the two brothers who had been so caring and thoughtful to one another. Every year, at the end of the harvest season, the fairies congregated around the monument and celebrated. On the monument, it was written,

"May my words be set before you like incense,
And my deeds be like the evening sacrifice."

باشد که گفتار و چون بخور کاهنان با درگاهت پذیرفته شود،

و رفتارم چون قربانی غروب

22

Delaram and the Harp

Once upon a day and once upon a time, under the purple dome of the sky, there was a very kind and beautiful girl called Delaram. She had learned how to sing and play the harp from her father. Her house was near a river surrounded by many big trees that reached the sky. Among the trees, there were nests full of beautiful birds. Delaram's voice was so beautiful and soothing that when she sang and played the harp, it made everyone happy. Even the birds started to sing and dance in the branches of the trees when she played.

One day, a young peri, called Parizad, was walking near Delaram's house. He heard her soothing voice and the lovely melody of her harp. He peered through the window and could see her great beauty. Parizad fell in love as though his heart was not one heart but a hundred hearts and wished to marry her. From that day on, he walked by her house every day.

One day, Delaram went to get water from the river. Parizad approached her and said, "Fair lady, I have heard you play the harp and sing with such beauty that it fills my heart with joy!" Delaram looked at Parizad and instantly fell in love with him.

But there was one problem. Parizad's mother loved her son deeply. She had taught him the lore of fairydom and had recited beautiful poems to him ever since he was a young peri. She had given him a special shirt made out of golden threads, and liked to see him wearing it while he played polo with his friends. Parizad's mother would never let her son marry a mere mortal! Her wish was that Parizad marry a fairy princess.

Parizad was so much in love with Delaram that he asked her to marry him without his mother's consent. Delaram agreed, and they were wed in secret shortly afterwards. After the ceremony, they went back to Parizad's home.

When Parizad was in the presence of his mother, he changed Delaram into a golden brooch to hide his new bride. He fashioned the brooch into the shape of a harp, and pinned it to the lapel of his shirt so that the beautiful Delaram could always be with him.

Days went by and Parizad and Delaram spent many happy times together. Parizad played polo with his friends, and Delaram loved to see him ride his horse and skillfully play the game. They sat among the trees where Delaram sang and played the harp, and Parizad was filled with joy.

One day, Parizad's mother became suspicious. She smelled Parizad's shirt and said,

> *"With what right, I shout,*
> *Is a human smell about?"*

She undid her son's magic and turned Delaram back to her human form. She saw the beautiful girl for the first time. Seeing such great beauty made her very jealous.

Every day, as soon as Parizad left the house, his mother gave Delaram hundreds of chores to do. The mean mother-in-law tried to wear her down and break her heart so that she would leave forever.

One day, Parizad's mother gave Delaram hundreds of dishes and hundreds of pots to wash until the end of the day. For every dish or pot that Delaram washed, Parizad's mother magically added a few more dirty ones. When Parizad returned home at the end of the day, he saw that Delaram was very tired and still washing dishes.

Parizad, who was also skillful in magic, made sure that all of the dishes and pots were cleaned and put away in a mere moment. When his mother came and checked on Delaram, she understood that her son had undone her magic. Angrily, she looked at Delaram and said,

> *"This work, you did not do,*
> *It is not what you were told,*
> *The work is from a peri,*
> *Whose shirt is made of gold!"*

Another day, Parizad's mother put hundreds of dirty clothes in front of Delaram and asked her to wash and dry and fold all of them by the end of the day. Delaram started washing the clothes, hanging them up in the sun and folding them. But as she worked, the mound of dirty clothes became bigger and bigger. At the end of the day, again Parizad came home and used his magic to instantly clean and dry and fold all of the clothes. Parizad's mother became angry again and told Delaram,

> *"This work, you did not do,*
> *It is not what you were told,*
> *The work is from a peri,*
> *Whose shirt is made of gold!"*

Parizad's mother realized that her son had the power to undo all of her magic. She went and consulted with one of her friends, a mean and nasty witch. The witch told her, "Find an excuse and send Delaram to my house so that I can imprison her in my witch's prison."

Parizad's mother came back and told Delaram, "I want to arrange a feast to honor you and your husband. At this feast, I will arrange a game of polo for Parizad and his friends to play in the fields near our house. You can sing and play your harp and I will prepare delicious food and sweet drinks. But our bucket has fallen inside of the well, like a heart fallen in sadness, and we need a special hook to bring it out. Please, go to my friend's house and get this special hook from her. Bring it back so that I can draw good water to make sweet drinks for the feast."

Delaram walked hours until she reached the witch's house. Outside, she saw a donkey that was very, very thin. The rope around the donkey's neck was so short that the poor creature could not reach a nearby mound of oats. Delaram felt sorry for the donkey, and brought the oats closer to him. She gave the donkey some water so that he could eat and drink freely. The poor thing ate and drank until he was satisfied.

Delaram saw a door that was open and it began to talk. "I am always open," said the door. "Please close me for a change!" it begged. Delaram entered the hallway and closed the always-opened door. Then she reached a door that was always closed that begged to be open. Delaram opened the door, went through it into a courtyard, and then kindly left it open behind her.

When she reached the courtyard, she saw the mean witch and asked her, "Can you please bring me a special hook for getting out the bucket from our well?" The witch brought the hook and gave it to her. Delaram politely thanked the witch and turned to go back home. The witch had prepared a magic potion to trap Delaram and sweetly asked, "Please sit down and have this delicious drink." Delaram felt a sudden sense of danger, and with hook in hand, began to run away.

The witch screamed, "Always-closed door! Stop Delaram from running away!" The always-closed door said to the witch, "You never opened me. Delaram was kind and opened me." The door let Delaram escape.

Then the witch screamed, "Always-opened door! Don't let Delaram escape!" The door answered, "You always left me open. You never paid any attention to me. Delaram was kind and closed me." It let Delaram escape.

Then the witch screamed, "Thin donkey! Run after Delaram and catch her!" The donkey said, "You always kept me hungry and thirsty. Delaram brought me oats and water." The donkey let Dalaram escape.

The farther Delaram ran away from the witch's house, the weaker and more powerless the witch became. As soon as Delaram reached home, the effect of the mean witch on Parizad's mother totally disappeared. It was as if Parizad's mother had woken up from a bad dream. She regretted all that she had done and asked for forgiveness.

Parizad's mother arranged a big feast for Parizad and Delaram. Parizad and his friends played polo in the fields. His mother served delicious food and sweet fragrant drinks. Delaram, more beautiful than any bride, played the harp and sang for all the guests. All the fairies remembered this feast for many, many years.

23

The Selfish Pussy Cat

Once upon a day and once upon a time, under the purple dome of the sky, there was a very kind and beautiful girl named Zibasteh. However, she had a problem. Her problem was that she was missing her thing to go wee-wee. Zibasteh had a fat lazy pussy cat that slept and ate all day, and had two things to go wee-wee. Zibasteh was very kind and gentle to her lazy pussy cat. When she needed to go wee-wee, she borrowed one of the things from her cat. But the pussy cat was very selfish. At times, the cat made her wait a long time, and demanded bigger and better rewards each time that Zibasteh needed to borrow it.

One day, Zibasteh and her mother went shopping in the city center. Suddenly, a number of horsemen with colorful flags came and announced, "The prince will soon be passing through. Go to the sides of the road and bow down as the prince's carriage goes by."

The prince had spent his time mainly in the palace and the only people he usually saw were the courtiers and guards. So, now that he had come out of the palace, he was very eager to see the outside world and all of the ordinary people.

As the prince's carriage passed by Zibasteh and her mother, the girl curiously looked up to catch a glimpse of the prince. At the same time that Zibasteh raised her head, he glanced out of the window and looked in her direction. He saw her beautiful face, and not with one heart but with a hundred hearts, fell in love with her.

"Stop the horses!" ordered the prince. The driver pulled on the reins of the fine white horses and the carriage stopped. The prince thought to himself, "I just saw the loveliest girl in the land, the loveliest I will ever see. I hope to find out who she is."

Zibasteh was worried that she had angered the prince's horsemen by raising her head. Afraid, she quickly ran back home with her mother. The prince ordered his horsemen to find the girl, but there was no sign of her anywhere.

When the prince got back to the palace, he told his father, "I have seen the most beautiful girl in this land. But when I stopped the carriage to find her, she was nowhere to be seen." The king ordered his courtiers, "Find the girl and bring her to the palace so that I can see her." The palace courtiers went to the city and knocked on every door, and asked if anyone knew anything about the beautiful girl.

They soon found the girl. Zibasteh, seeing the courtiers at the door, began shaking in fear. The courtiers calmed her down and said, "The prince has fallen in love with you and wants your hand in marriage." Zibasteh started to worry. She was too embarrassed to tell them of her problems and said, "I am not worthy of marrying the prince. We are a poor family." The courtiers answered, "This does not matter to the prince." Zibasteh made another excuse, and said, "My mother is old and needs me to care for her." The courtiers said, "The prince will provide your family with all that is needed."

Zibasteh, running out of excuses, told them, "I have a pussy cat that I love very much. She is always with me and I wouldn't know what to do without her." The courtiers couldn't understand why Zibasteh was making so many excuses. They were concerned that the king would be angry if they didn't bring her back, and said, "Nothing can undo the king's order. Take the pussycat with you, and come with us to the palace where the king and prince are waiting for you." So, Zibasteh took her pussycat and went with the courtiers to the palace.

When they reached the palace, the king took one look at the kind face of the girl. He was happy with the prince's choice, and gave his blessing for Zibasteh to wed his son. He ordered his courtiers to arrange a big wedding and invite many guests.

The selfish pussy cat, seeing the luxury of the palace, snootily put her nose up in the air, and told Zibasteh, "From now on, I want bigger and better rewards, or else I will not lend you my thing." "What is it that you want?" asked the frightened girl. "I want some of the fancy food that they will give to you," the cat mewed disdainfully. The girl agreed. "And I want to be petted and groomed and combed for many hours every day," the cat said haughtily. The girl agreed. "And I want you to wash and clean my fur, and cut it when it grows too long so that I will be comfortable," the pussycat sneered in contempt.

Zibasteh needed the pussycat for the wedding night, and said, "I will agree to all of your demands on one condition; on our wedding night, you will lend me your thing and not bother me or the prince until dawn." The cat agreed that on the day of the wedding, she would give Zibasteh her thing and not ask for it back until dawn.

It was a beautiful wedding with delicious food and delectable sweets. People danced to merry music, clicking their heels on the floor throughout the night. Many guests were there, wishing the young couple a lifetime of happiness. Little did they know that Zibasteh was nervous and anxious because she was afraid that the selfish cat would not keep her promise.

The prince eventually took Zibasteh to the bridle chamber. The pussycat followed them, running after the new bride. Zibasteh took the pussycat and stroked her fur. The selfish cat began to whine and fret. The cat whispered into Zibasteh's ear and demanded, "I have decided not to let you keep my thing till the morning. Return it back to me right now!" Shaken, Zibasteh put the cat down, and started to cry.

The prince saw her tears and came to comfort his new bride. He wisely saw that the cat was bothering her. He drew his sword out of his sheath and swiftly "killed the cat at the bridal chamber". It was known from then on, that it is always very important to solve a problem before it gets out of hand. Zibasteh never lacked for anything ever again. The prince, Zibasteh, and their children lived happily ever after.

24

The Wizard and the Shepherd

Once upon a day and once upon a time, under the purple dome of the sky, there was a wise wizard who had a clever son. One day, the wizard's son asked him, "Why do some people have so much to eat and are wasteful, and some don't have enough food to eat at all?" The wizard told his son, "I will take you outside of the city and you will find the answer for yourself."

They reached a mountain at the outskirts of the city. The wizard said, "On top of this mountain, there is an old man who lives in a house with one room. In the small courtyard of his house, there is a walnut tree and a well. The tree produces one walnut every day, which the old man eats to keep alive. I will fill the branches of this tree with many walnuts and make the well overflow with water. Then we will go together and pay him a visit so that we can eat one or two nuts and have a sip of water."

The wizard waved his magic wand and spoke some magic words. He told his son, "I have now made the old man's tree so full of walnuts that it is bent over, and his water has risen so fast that it is now dripping over the edge of the well."

As the wizard and his son were walking towards the one-room house, the old man saw that his tree had suddenly been blessed with many nuts. He gathered them all and put them in a bin in his room. He looked at his well and saw that it was overflowing. He took a pail and filled it with water, and also hid it in his room.

The wizard and his son reached the old man's house and knocked on the door. The old man opened the door half-way and looked at them suspiciously. The wizard said, "We have been walking for a long time in the heat to reach the top of this mountain and my young son is very thirsty. Could you spare a sip of water?"The old man answered, "I'm a poor old man. I wish I had some water or food to offer you." After the wizard and his son left, the old man went into his room. He saw that a fat mouse had entered the bin and was busy chewing one of the walnuts.

The wizard and his son walked down the mountain, and reached a green field with a river flowing through. They saw a shepherd with a large herd of sheep. The wizard waved his magic wand and spoke some magic words. There came a strong wind and scattered the sheep in all directions.

The shepherd tried to stop the sheep from running away. He knew that there was a nearby forest where the wolves howled. He knew that there were peaks nearby where mountain goats with sharp horns angrily butted any creature passing through. He knew that there were strong currents in the river that could take the sheep far upstream. The shepherd spent a long time trying to gather his sheep, but could only find a few of them. Tired, he finally sat down near the riverbank and drank some water.

The wizard and his son came close by. As soon as the shepherd saw them, he shouted, "Dear friends! Come, let us sit down and eat together. When food is shared, hunger is not. Please be my guests." The shepherd took out his bundle of food and opened it. Inside, there were a few thin slices of bread, and a small amount of leftover sheep cheese. He offered all that he had to his guests. Then he turned to his few remaining sheep, milked them, and gave the wizard and his son the fresh milk.

Soon, some villagers passed by. They looked very tired and hungry, and the shepherd invited them to eat together. He said, "When food is shared, hunger is not." The wizard performed his magic once again, and there was enough bread and cheese for everybody.

The wizard and his son thanked the shepherd and bid him farewell. When they were far way, the wizard waved his wand and spoke some magic words. From every corner, all of the sheep came back to the shepherd. A faithful dog joined the herd and took care of them from that day on.

The old man ate one walnut a day, the shepherd always had plenty of food, and the boy had learned a good lesson.

25

Journey to the Land of Darkness

Once upon a day and once upon a time, under the purple dome of the sky, there was a very strong and courageous young man. He and his friends decided to travel to the Land of Darkness. The young man had an old father who was very wise, but was now frail and lean, and could not walk easily. The old man spent most of his time reading and talking to friends, as many old men do. In his younger years, when he walked upright and had broad shoulders and a full head of dark wavy hair, he had traveled the world, which made him not only wise, but also worldly.

When the father heard of his son's plans, he cautioned, "The journey you are about to take is treacherous and full of danger. You will need a prudent and careful guide to help you travel and return safely." The son told his father, "After I come back from this journey, I will be wiser and more experienced, like you, but you are right. If there are dangers that I am not aware of, it could cost us our lives." The father advised, "Hide me in the back of your carriage. Every now and then, come and listen to what I have to say."

The young man and his group of friends prepared for their journey. They packed many bags with ample provisions, and put them into their carriages. The young man hid his old father in the back of his carriage among the stored luggage. The group of friends started on their way to the Land of Darkness, pulled by the finest and strongest horses.

When the travelers came close to the Land of Darkness, the old father whispered to his son, "Tell your friends to take the horseshoes off of the horses. This land is like a big magnet. If the horseshoes are not removed, the metal will stick to the ground, and the horses will not be able to go onward." The young man relayed the message to his friends, without telling them that these were his father's words.

Some in the group readily agreed and promptly removed the horseshoes from their horses. Others snickered and scoffed and did not heed his words. The young man tried to convince his friends that the idea was worthy, without divulging the source of his newfound wisdom. He told them, "I have learned from wise men that there is a difference between ordinary lands and those that have deep earthly forces from within."

As the group moved forward, the days became darker and darker, and the magnetic force in this strange land became stronger and stronger. The friends who listened to the warning, and had taken off the horseshoes, continued traveling easily. The horses whose stubborn riders had not taken off their horseshoes moved slower and slower, until their hooves were stuck to the cold ground and could move no more.

They reached a road that was full of rocks. The father again whispered to his son from his hiding place, "Tell your friends to take some of the rocks, not too many, and not too few, and load them into their carriages. Those who take too little will be regretful, and those who take too many will be sorry as well." The young man told his friends, "Let us take some rocks, but not too many and not too few."

Some of his friends laughed at the idea, and didn't take any rocks at all. Some of his friends took so many rocks that their horses could barely hold the load. But some of his friends listened to him and took just a few rocks.

Those who took no rocks continued traveling easily and galloped forward. Those who took too many rocks overloaded their horses, could not continue, and stayed behind. But those who took only a few rocks travelled without difficultly, and maintained a steady, even pace.

They came upon a thick, dark forest and the old man again whispered to his son, "Tell your friends to be very careful passing through these woods. Some of the trees have poisonous snakes resting on their branches. Some bear fruits that you will need to collect for eating on the long journey ahead. Tell them to be careful about which trees they choose because there are sneaky snakes that sleep on branches full of fruit."

As usual, some of his friends didn't heed the wise warning of the old father. Impatient and greedy, they climbed the trees without looking, and faced frightening snakes instead of delicious fruit! Some of his friends went along their merry way and were too lazy to pick any fruit at all, thinking that they had enough food packed away in their provisions. But those who were wise and patient cautiously picked fruits from good trees, and had ample food for the rest of the journey.

One day, when it was so dark that they could barely see anything, the father told his son in a low whisper, "Tell your friends that we are now in the depth of darkness. In order to find the way out, they can no longer rely on their eyesight. They must pay attention to the slightest of sounds, even the quietest ones. They must be aware of every scent they smell. And most importantly, they must not let fear stop them from continuing on their way."

Those who let fear overcome them traveled so deeply into the Land of Darkness that they began to think dark thoughts, and dream dark dreams, and soon lost their way. Those who did not pay attention to the sounds and scents took a wrong turn in the road, and went astray. But those who were aware of all that was around them continued on without fear. With the help of the old father, his courageous son and the remaining friends gradually came out of the darkness into the light of day, and eventually reached home.

Those who had taken rocks from the Land of Darkness looked and saw that they had brought back the biggest, most beautiful diamonds that could ever be found. They sold them and became very rich. More importantly, all who had gone on the journey and returned safely were wiser and more experienced in the ways of the world. As the years passed, some would guide their own sons through the Land of Darkness – carefully hidden in the back of a carriage.

26

Fatemeh Nesa

Once upon a day and once upon a time, under the purple dome of the sky, there was a woman who lived in a village near the river and washed clothes for a living. She had a faithful donkey and two children – a beautiful daughter called Fatemeh Nesa, and a well-mannered son with no hair, called Faisal the Bald. Fatemeh Nesa and Faisal were very close and liked each other very much.

One day, the mother loaded her donkey with a bundle of clothes to wash, and went with her daughter to the edge of the river. The donkey had a fine bell around his neck, and every step of the way you could hear, "ding dong, ding dong." The donkey secretly sang in his heart,

> "Ding dong, ding dong, we're on our way,
> Ding dong, on a stony road we'll stay,
> With Fatemeh we'll ride away."

When they reached the river's edge, the mother looked for a good place to wash the clothes. Meanwhile, her daughter had wandered far off to play. The mother called out, "Fatemeh Nesa! Fatemeh

Nesa!" But there was no answer. The mother looked all around, but could not see her daughter anywhere.

The donkey, realizing that Fatemeh Nesa was lost, started to run and gallop, ringing the bell around his neck and shouted,

> *"Ding dong, they took my Fatemeh away,*
> *Ding dong, they ate my clover and hay."*

The worried mother called the donkey. She quickly got on his back, and swiftly rode home. "Faisal, my dear son," she cried, "your sister is missing!" Faisal calmed down his poor mother and said, "I know a sparrow that has been my friend since childhood. She can help us find Fatemeh Nesa."

Faisal ran to the sparrow's nest and cried out, "Dear clever sparrow, my sister is lost! Please help me find her." The sparrow answered, "I will help you if you share your food with me." Faisal said, "I have some sugar beets that have been cooking the whole night over charcoal. They are sweet and delicious. I will share all of my sugar beets with you."

Faisal brought out the sugar beets and they started eating lunch together. But for every peck the sparrow took, Faisal the Bald took a big, big bite. The sparrow complained,

> *"One little peck for me, one big bite for you,*
> *This way I can't be full, so can't we share for two?"*

Faisal apologized and gave the sparrow big chunks of food to eat.

When the sparrow was well fed, Faisal asked her, "How can we find Fatemeh Nesa?" The sparrow answered, "I will fly above and ask the other birds if they have seen where she was taken. When I find out, I will come back and show you the way."

The sparrow flew away, and came back after some time and said to Faisal, "Your sister has been taken to a fortress of the ghouls. In that fortress, there is a ghoul so young that it does not yet have horns or a tail. This young ghoul has fallen in love with your sister and wants to marry her without her consent!"

This made Faisal very worried. The thought of a ghoul marrying his sister frightened him, especially the idea that he would have nieces and nephews with horns and tails. Faisal asked the sparrow anxiously, "Where is the ghoul's fortress?" The bird said, "I will fly high in the air and show you the way. Ride your donkey and follow where I fly."

Faisal rode the donkey with the bell and they hurried away. The donkey cried,

> "Ding dong, Fatemeh was taken away.
> Ding dong, they took her far, far away.
> Ding dong, the nasty ghouls we'll fight,
> And free Fatemeh from her nasty plight!"

Faisal rode on the donkey for a long time and followed the clever sparrow flying high in the sky. Finally, the bird swooped down near a river and said, "I can see the fortress in the distance. Let us rest and eat here." They sat down and Faisal took out his sweet sugar beets. Again, Faisal the Bald took big bites of the food and left the sparrow with only small pecks to eat. The sparrow complained,

> "One little peck for me, one big bite for you,
> This way I can't be full. Can't we share for two?"

The donkey, also tired and hungry, chimed in,

> "Big bites for you, but I have no oats,
> So how can you ask me to run like a goat?"

Faisal gave a large piece of sugar beet to the sparrow. Then, he took a bag of oats from the donkey's back and put it in front of him so that he could eat.

When they were all fed and rested, Faisal asked the sparrow, "How can I get into the fortress and free my sister from the ghoul with no horn and no tail?" The sparrow answered, "I will show you how to get into the fortress. But before you enter, we must find the magic talisman."

Faisal asked, "What talisman?" The sparrow answered, "In old times, a wise and pure-hearted craftsman made a small talisman on which he engraved forty prayers. If you find the talisman and say even one of the prayers aloud, its magic will be released, and the ghouls will lose their power and fall.

"Where can I find this magic talisman?" asked Faisal. The sparrow pecked on some more sugar beet and said, "The ghouls were so afraid of this talisman that they asked a mean witch to take it and hide it in a cave near the top of a high mountain. She did so, and the ghouls put a huge stone to block the entrance of the cave. But I know of a secret opening, and can go into the cave and bring the talisman to you."

The sun was setting in the west and it began to get dark. "We will continue early tomorrow morning," said Faisal, who was now sleepy and tired. They found a comfortable corner to rest for the night.

At dawn, the sparrow flew to the high mountaintop and reached the cave. The little bird entered the secret opening, grabbed the talisman, and brought it back to Faisal.

Later that morning, when the sun brightened the earth, the ghouls, like they did every day, left their fortress. As soon as they did, the sparrow led Faisal and the donkey into the ghoul's fortress. Upon entering, Faisal put his hand into his pocket and felt the magic talisman, which eased his fears. They quickly began searching to find Faisal's missing sister.

After looking for some time, they found a dark room in the basement. It had a small window with iron bars, and a huge iron door with a big lock. Faisal peered through the window, and saw Fatemeh Nesa along with other unfortunate prisoners. Happy to see his sister, Faisal cried out to her, "I have come to free you!" Fatemeh Nesa cried back, "These ghouls are very cruel and dangerous. If they catch you here, they will take you and imprison you here forever! Run away!" Faisal calmed his sister down and said, "Don't worry. I have a magic talisman in my pocket that makes the ghouls weak and powerless."

Meanwhile, the clever sparrow looked this way and that way, to the right and to the left, up and down, and saw a crevice high up in the wall. She flew up to the crevice and sure enough, found the key hidden there. But the key was too heavy for the little bird, so Faisal came and stood on the donkey's back, reached up, and took it. He quickly jumped down, opened the big lock, and freed Fatemeh Nesa and all of the other prisoners.

They quickly ran out of the fortress, but just as they ran through the main door, one of the biggest and ugliest ghouls saw them escaping, and started shouting in a rage,

> "I scream and shout,
> I smell a human about."

Faisal brought the talisman out of his pocket and held it out with a strong arm in the face of the giant ugly ghoul. He uttered one of the engraved prayers out loud. The big ghoul started to shake and tremble. Its ugly face turned pale and pasty. Its disgusting left eye suddenly closed shut. And then it fell on the ground with a loud thump. The other ghouls came closer to see what happened to the big ugly ghoul, and the same thing happened to them! A few of the ghouls saw this from afar, and were so afraid that they turned around and ran away to a faraway land. Even the young ghoul with no horns and no tail, who wanted to marry Fatemeh Nesa, was frightened of the talisman, and ran away!

The sparrow showed everyone the way back. They reached their homes and their loved ones, and were never bothered by any ghoul ever again. Fatemeh Nesa stayed close to her mother on their way to the river. As for Faisal, he was never called Faisal the Bald again because he always shared food with the sparrow and others in need, and gave his donkey plenty of clover and oats.

27

The Happy Bricklayer

Once upon a day and once upon a time, under the purple dome of the sky, there was a strong young bricklayer, who was always happy and enjoyed his work. He sang as he worked hard, and always had a smile on his face. This made the other workers around him feel good and happy too.

One day, two merchants passed by the building site where the happy young bricklayer was working. They always argued and made bets, and wanted to prove their point of view to the other. As they passed by the happy worker, the younger merchant said to the older one, "I think people like him are always happy from the day they were born." The older merchant replied, "No, it is the way they live and the people around them that make them happy." They argued for a long while and then, to prove who was right, decided to make a bet.

The old merchant, believing happiness could be made, said, "I bet that I can make this bricklayer so unhappy, and so sad, and so forlorn that he will slow down at work and hate it. And then, I'll make him even happier than he is now." The young merchant, who thought that people were happy from birth, said, "I don't think that this is possible. I'll bet you that you can't do it." So, they shook hands and bet on ten gold coins.

The older merchant told one of his assistants to go and find out how the bricklayer lives. The assistant was a bright man. He went and talked to the neighbors and asked many questions. Then, he came back to the old merchant and reported, "This is the way the bricklayer lives. He has a beautiful wife, who loves him very much. Every day, when he comes back from work, she prepares hot water so that he can wash himself, brings him clean clothes, and serves him tasty food that she has prepared. She is loving and soothing and very kind to her husband. The bricklayer returns her love. He brings her presents and tries to make her happy all of the time. He sings to her and tells her funny stories. There is much laughter and joy in their house. They also have good friends and meet with them every now and again."

The old merchant made a plan. He sent one of his workers to the bricklayer's building site and told him to befriend the happy worker. The old merchant also sent a woman, who had worked in his house, to become friendly with the bricklayer's wife.

The old merchant's worker struck up a friendship with the young bricklayer and gained his confidence. Then he told him, "I'm sorry, I have bad news for you. While you are working so hard, others have seen your wife with another man." Meanwhile, the woman worker said to the bricklayer's wife, "While you are preparing food and warming up water for your husband, he is not at work and with another woman."

The first few days, the bricklayer and his wife ignored what they had heard. As days went by, the two workers of the old merchant repeated their lies over and over again. Little by little, doubt entered the bricklayer's heart. At night he could not sleep well, and in the day he could not eat in peace. When he was at work, he couldn't concentrate on his job. He became sadder and sadder as each day passed. The wife became so sad and worried that she had no desire to cook. She did not warm up water for her husband and had no patience to even talk to him.

The old merchant called the young merchant and showed how sad the bricklayer had become, and how slowly he now laid the bricks. The young merchant couldn't believe his eyes and felt sorry for the poor young man. He implored the old merchant to change his circumstances back to the way things were before. The old merchant said, "Now, as I said in my bet, I will make him happier than ever." The old merchant called his two workers and told them, "Go back to the bricklayer and his wife, and try to bring harmony back into their lives."

The merchant's assistant went to the bricklayer and apologized, "Forgive me. By mistake, I thought another woman was your wife. I asked around, and all of the neighbors and friends said that your dear wife is very kind and faithful and loving to you."

The woman worker also went back and apologized to the wife. She said, "Please forgive me. I've made a terrible mistake. The man I thought was your husband was someone else. Without thinking, I reached the wrong conclusion. Your dear husband, the bricklayer, is known everywhere as the most faithful and loving husband."

When the husband came home that night, he brought his wife a present. He sang to her and told her funny stories. She had prepared hot water for him. After he washed himself, she brought him clean clothes. She set the table and served delicious aromatic food. The husband and wife were happy that their doubts had been proven baseless. Their hearts were cleansed from all sadness, and they were reunited once more. This made the bricklayer happy and strong. He went to work full of energy, and made everyone around him happy again. His wife was even more loving and kind than before.

The young merchant handed over ten gold coins to the older merchant and said, "You have won the bet!" The old merchant decided to give the young couple a present that would make them even happier. He bought a beautiful and expensive house that was very comfortable in a good neighborhood of the city. With the help of his assistants, he sold the house to the bricklayer at a very low price. The bricklayer and his wife lived there happily for many years, and raised many happy children.

28

Two Friends and the Magic Wand

Once upon a day and once upon a time, under the purple dome of the sky, there were two boys who always played together. One was called Gershasb, who was very strong and curious. The other was called Borzuy, who was very bright and knew many languages. They were such good friends that when one shot an arrow, the other knew where it would land.

When they grew older, Gershasb said to Borzuy, "Let's travel around the world and see as many cities as we can." Borzuy readily agreed and they packed some food and water, and set out to see the world with no fear in their hearts.

They first came upon a city near the sea. There, they watched fishermen in big boats catching fish in their big nets. Some caught many fish and some only a few. Borzuy said to Gershasb, "A good fisherman neither fishes too close to the seashore nor too far away from it."

They continued travelling and reached a city at the peak of a mountain range. There, they saw horsemen who skillfully rode their large fine horses on snakelike, winding mountain paths. The horse riders played exciting games, competing against one another and showing off their skills. There were those who won, and those who lost. Gershasb said to Borzuy, "To win a horse race, the horse must be one with the rider."

Continuing on, the friends reached a city by the river. There, they met some upright and polite people, who were famous for their scrumptious cooking. The two young men ate the finest dishes of fish, and enjoyed the most fragrant, delicious deserts. Borzuy said, "The meals prepared by master chefs entice you with aroma, but a meal prepared by a mother is full of the fragrance of love."

They reached a city in a faraway place, where each house was cut into the face of the mountains. At night, a light flickered inside each home, and in the orchard of the sky, the stars shone like silver sequins. Gershasb looked up and said, "God created the universe and men made cities." They left the city at dawn just as the stars were becoming fainter and fainter.

Gershasb and Borzuy travelled on, and came upon a city full of beautiful trees and brightly colored flowers, dotted with many fine sculptures. Every building was like a work of art. In the middle of the city square, there was a resplendent statue of a man riding a horse. Borzuy said, "Heroes, such as these, are the fathers of their people."

Finally, they reached the ruins of a city of ancient times. Parts of the city were untouched and well-kept, as beautiful as they had ever been, and parts had crumbled completely. The buildings and walls of the city had been made of big stone blocks, chiseled with writings of old times.

They saw a narrow passageway, where many would not have gone. They entered the passageway and walked for some time until they reached a dim courtyard surrounded by high stone walls.

In the middle of the courtyard, there stood a large statue of a cow. On the wall behind it, there were writings of ancient times. Borzuy translated the writings, which said,

> *"When the sun shines on the cow three times,*
> *the gate will open wide."*

The surrounding walls were so high that the sun's rays could barely reach the statue. All was dark, except a tiny spot of light that landed on one of the writings. Gershasb turned around and saw a small opening in the wall behind him. He noticed a thin ray of sunshine beaming through it. He waited and watched some more. As the sun moved across the sky, the spot of light moved slightly upwards, as though it were trying to give him a message. As more time passed, the spot inched closer and closer to the cow. Eventually, it landed on the cow's horn, encircling it with light. Gershasb touched the statue's horn and played with it. He discovered that if he pulled it hard enough, the horn would move.

Gershasb shouted to Borzuy excitedly,

> *"The meaning of three times is that we should move this*
> *horn three times in three different directions!"*

Gershasb grasped the horn, and with all of his might, moved it up towards the sky. They heard a loud sound of large stone slabs sliding against each other. Then, Gershasb took the horn again, and with all of his might, moved it downwards, like into the depths of the deep sea. They heard a softer sound of stones rolling down. Gershasb grabbed the horn for the third time, and with all of his might, returned it to its original position. It was as though nothing had ever happened. But to their surprise, a stone gate in the wall behind them opened wide, revealing a very dark passageway.

Fearlessly, the young men carefully entered. Their eyes soon got used to the darkness, just as one gets used to the night. Finally, they reached a small room with a platform at its center. They looked closer and found a small wand lying there. Borzuy picked it up, and noticed some writing on it, but the room was so dark that it was impossible to see what was written. The two friends made their way out of the darkness back to the courtyard.

Now in the light, Borzuy looked at the wand and deciphered the ancient writings. It said,

"When a good deed is yours, the rain of blessing pours."

The sun was setting and the cold wind of autumn began to blow strongly. It became darker and the first stars of the night flickered in the purple sky. Borzuy and Gershasb left the ruins and went to find an inn to spend the night.

The morning after, they continued on their journey. By mid-day, they reached another city. At the gate of the city, they saw an old man who was thirsty, helplessly begging for water. Gershasb opened his flask of water and filled the beggar's bowl until it was full. The thankful old man hastily drank the water, and asked, "What has brought you here?" Gershasb answered, "We are two friends travelling around the world to see many cities." The old man stared at them incredulously and said, "This city has suffered a drought for many years. It has been a long time since anyone has come to visit here. Water is so scarce that nobody shares it with anyone else."

Gershasb and Borzuy passed through the gate and entered the city. All of the trees were dry and without leaves. No flowers could be seen. There was no sign of greenery.

Borzuy felt the wand moving. He took it out of his knapsack and held it firmly. As they were walking, the magic wand unexpectedly moved and pointed in another direction. The two friends followed the wand until they came upon a dry well.

Suddenly, the wand flew out of Borzuy's hand, and it fell right into the well! Magically, the well filled with so much water that it began to overflow. Passers-by saw the water gushing out, and shouted with joy. The news of the overflowing well soon spread throughout the city. People rushed to get water. They first let the children and the helpless drink, and then, they themselves drank.

Soon after, the first rain of autumn came. It washed the city and the surrounding fields until the dry lands were thirsty no longer. That year, the city was blessed with heavy rainfall. Early in the spring, the trees started to bud, and the fields were green and covered with blankets of wild flowers.

Gershasb and Borzuy saw the new beauty of the city and decided to travel no more. They found two kind and gentle sisters to marry, and lived there happily.

The city grew into one of the most visited cities of the world. Every spring, people came to see the beauty of its trees and flowers. As for the magic wand, it stayed in the well forever.

29

The Twin Princes

Once upon a day and once upon a time, under the purple dome of the sky, there was a king who had identical twin sons. His greatest worry was which one would become king after he leaves this great earth. He consulted the wise men of the palace. They suggested having a great tournament in order to choose the heir to the throne. The wise men continued, "Whoever wins will be proclaimed as the next king". So a tournament was arranged by heroes of the army, who were masters of horse-riding, sword-fighting, and archery.

There was much pomp and circumstance as the games began. The squares in the palace were decorated with colorful flags and purple banners ornamented with gold. A grand procession of the royal uniformed guards was led by the great trumpeters of the court. Following the opening ceremonies, the king declared that the tournament was now open.

The tournament lasted three days. The first day started with horse-riding competitions. The brothers rode mighty horses, and skillfully jumped over hurdles. They raced their horses at high speed through a zigzagged course to get to the finish line. Both finished at the same time, without knocking down any of the hurdles.

On the second day, there was sword-fighting. The brothers took mighty swords and battled each other to see who could nick the other's clothes, but no one could touch the other. The king's best swordsman, who carefully judged the brothers, declared a tie.

On the third day, the competition turned to archery. Some targets were placed high up, some were placed low down, some were on the left, and some were on the right. Each contestant had to shoot at all of them while riding on a swift horse. The two princes were equally skillful, and all of their arrows landed exactly at the center of each target.

Later on in the day, they had to show their prowess at shooting targets so far away that it was hardly possible to see them. The first prince raised his bow and arrow and hit the center of the target again and again. The second prince did the same. However, on the last and final shot, he felt a sudden pain in his arm and flinched. The arrow went high up into the sky and was never seen again.

Even though the prince was saddened by his defeat, he accepted his fate. The king announced the winning son as the rightful heir to the throne, and the other as the high commander of the army.

As years went by, the king became old and eventually passed into the heavens above. The heir to the throne became king, and his brother served as his loyal commander-in-chief.

In the neighboring land, there was a cruel caliph who always waged wars and tried to conquer the surrounding lands. He was so cruel that all of his servants and courtiers of the palace were afraid of him, and all of his soldiers hated him. He would imprison his subjects for little or no reason. One of the prisoners was a wise and good-natured wizard, who was locked up in the castle prison. The wizard knew the twin princes, and in the past was a close friend of the late king.

Hearing that the old king had finally passed away, the cruel caliph thought, "The new king is inexperienced. This is a good opportunity to attack the neighboring county and conquer it." He called the head of the army to prepare for war.

The news of the invading army reached the ears of the young king. He consulted with his brother and wise ministers. The minister of the right hand said, "There is no choice. We have to act quickly and defeat the army of the enemy." The minister of the left hand said, "We have to force them to retreat back to their miserable caliph." The king's brother, the commander-in-chief, wisely said, "It is not enough to make the enemy retreat. We have to throw this cruel caliph out of his castle and free the people from his evil ways."

At night, the king's mighty army, led by his courageous twin brother, started to move forward. The soldiers swiftly rode their horses and confronted the invading army before dawn. Surprised, and without the urge to protect their mean caliph, the soldiers soon scattered in every direction.

The king's brother led his army to the castle of the cruel caliph. The palace guards, seeing such a mighty army approaching the palace, knelt down and surrendered. The castle was now in the hands of the commander-in-chief. He ordered his soldiers to arrest the cruel caliph and imprison him. When they went to the palace prison, they were astonished to see so many forlorn and forgotten prisoners languishing in jail. They quickly freed them all.

The good-natured wizard was freed along with all of the other prisoners. He asked the soldiers to take him to their commander.

When the prince saw the wizard, he recognized him as the good old friend of his late father. The wizard said, "The cruel caliph did not know that good magic could escape from the walls of his prison." Puzzled, the prince asked, "What do you mean?" The wizard continued, "In the tournament between you and your dear brother, the pain that you felt in your arm while drawing the bow was not accidental. You will forgive me, but this pain was caused by my good magic to lead you here and free this land."

The commander became king of the land that he had freed. The two brothers reigned over their neighboring countries in peace and tranquility for many, many years, and were known as "the two righteous kings".

30

Blanket-Ears and Waq-Waqs

Once upon a day and once upon a time under the purple dome of the sky, there was a seafarer who was very bold. He had reached places in the heart of the sea that nobody before him had ever discovered, and had seen creatures that nobody before him had ever seen. On his ship, there were hardy experienced sailors, who in wind and rain and storm were fearlessly ready to help. There was also a wise old traveler on board, who knew many languages and could converse easily with the locals wherever he went.

One day, the ship reached an island full of exotic creatures. Their faces were like those of innocent children. Their clothes were made of leaves, beautifully colored like the first leaves of spring. Their feet were like the roots of trees. When they talked among themselves, it sounded as if little dogs were barking, with a sound like "Waq-Waq".

The traveler approached the creatures and listened carefully to their conversation. Soon, he could understand that they were speaking a real language, and realized that they could talk about everything.

The seafarer told the wise traveler, "Ask these creatures who they are and what this island is called." So, the creatures of the island told their story:

"We are called Waq-Waqs and this place is called Waq-Waq Island. We are half human and half tree. Many years ago, we lived a long, happy, and joyful life. Every year, on the very first day of spring, each Waq-Waq would sprout one and only one beautiful fragrant flower, which blossomed from our hearts. As soon as the flower opened, it filled us with joy, and let our human half take over so that we could move freely throughout the land.

Then one day, an evil witch came and demanded that we become as cruel as she was, but we did not agree to do so. She cursed us, and put a spell on the island, and made the soil impure. Being half-tree, this wilted our heartfelt flowers and shortened our lives."

The seafarer told the wise traveler, "Tell the Waq-Waqs that if they wish, we can take them away to the Jungle of Blanket-Ears." The traveler told the Waq-Waqs all about the jungle, and they listened carefully to his words:

"The Jungle of Blanket-Ears is in a faraway land. It is so far away, that to reach there, one has to go all the way to China and beyond. In this jungle, like in any jungle, there are big leafy trees, and colorful singing birds, and animals of every kind.

But there are also other creatures that are very different, and these are called Blanket-Ears. Blanket-Ears are kind and gentle beings with very large ears, even larger than those of an elephant. They are very skillful at climbing up tall trees and jumping from one branch to the other.

During the day, they jump from tree to tree to find tasty fruits to eat, with their ears flinging in flight. At night, as the cold breeze blows through the large leafy branches, they put one of their long ears on a branch underneath their bodies on which to sleep, and use the other ear as a soft, warm blanket to cover themselves.

Blanket-Ears are the guardians of the jungle and they always keep the jungle fresh and green. Their tongues can dissolve anything that they lick, and at times, when a branch of a tree becomes too dry, all of the Blanket-Ears gather around and lick the dry branch until it falls. In this way, the jungle is always full of fresh, beautiful trees.

Blanket-Ears dislike fighting and are very peaceful. They are very thoughtful, and always ready to help others. Of all the creatures that I have ever seen, they are the purest and gentlest of all."

When the Waq-Waqs heard about the Jungle of Blanket-Ears, they agreed to go there, and boarded the ship. On their journey, the Waq-Waqs listened to many adventures of the seafarer, and the wise traveler translated them all. They heard stories of different lands and many creatures. On the one hand they wished to see the world like the seafarer and the traveler, but on the other hand, they wished to be able to one day return to Waq-Waq Island.

The Waq-Waqs finally reached the jungle. After meeting Blanket-Ears, they settled in a corner of the jungle. Many months passed. Autumn came and went. And after that, came the winter rains, which rejuvenated the Waq-Waqs. They started to live longer and longer, just like in olden times. Now that spring had come, the Waq-Waqs started to flower again, and turned the corner of the jungle into a fragrant and wondrous place.

One fine spring night, a nasty evil witch was passing through the jungle, and spotted a beautiful flower sprouting from a small Waq-Waq's heart. In an instant, she clutched the flower in her bony fingers and plucked it from the small unfortunate creature's breast. The stricken Waq-Waq yelped in pain. The witch quickly ran away, cackling and screaming. She shouted with glee, "What a lovely magic wand the stem of this flower will make, and what lovely evil will come of it!"

Without his flower, the poor Waq-Waq could no longer move freely, and stayed in one place like a tree. Ever since that fateful night, he became ill-tempered and was rude to everyone. As time passed, his behavior became worse and worse. He took stones from the ground, and threw them at others. He barked and scared any innocent creatures of the jungle that passed nearby.

Little by little, the stricken Waq-Waq became so unruly that all of the other Waq-Waqs could not bear him any longer, and moved away. The colorful singing birds of the jungle did not fly nearby, and the other animals stayed far, far away. The surrounding beautiful flowers dried out. Soon, the ill-behaved Waq-Waq was left all alone.

Blanket-Ears, who were the guardians of the jungle, saw the devastation of this once beautiful part of the jungle, and grew very anxious. The eldest of the Blanket-Ears thought, "Because of this wild and unruly Waq-Waq, an entire corner of this magical, beautiful jungle has become empty of trees. If this goes on, I'm afraid that the whole jungle may disappear." So he called a meeting of all Blanket-Ears to gather on the branches of a huge tree in the middle of the jungle.

At the meeting, the eldest Blanket-Ear asked the others what should be done. A young Blanket-Ear said, "This Waq-Waq should be punished!" Others disagreed and an argument ensued, which became more and more heated. For the first time ever, Blanket-Ears were fighting with one another. The witch, who was hiding nearby, heard them arguing, and became very happy.

Suddenly, Homa, the rare bird that never stops flying, was spotted overhead, which surprised everyone. Wherever Homa flew, peace and tranquility soon followed. All Blanket-Ears became quiet and stopped fighting. Homa said, "The evil witch has brought this upon you. The angrier you become, the stronger she will be."

Then, Homa flew towards the witch. Unaffected by her wicked magic, the great bird snatched the evil wand away, and took it to the high mountains where fires always burn. There, he opened his claws, and dropped the wand into the flames.

One of the wisest of Blanket-Ears turned to the others and said, "If hate and anger has caused this corner of the jungle to become dry, we should all join together and plant new trees around the ill-tempered Waq-Waq. When the trees are small, he will not be able reach them. When they get big and their roots become stronger, their branches will inch closer to him and eventually make him feel better." They all agreed that this was the best thing to do.

The Blanket-Ears went to different corners of the jungle, and freed the roots of tiny trees from the earth. They brought the small trees and planted them near the wild Waq-Waq. The trees grew taller and taller, and were soon full of green leaves. New flowers sprung up everywhere, and the colorful birds that sang so beautifully began to return.

The beautiful branches inched closer and closer to the Waq-Waq. At first, he growled when a small branch swept past his pain-stricken and swollen chest on the spot where his beautiful flower had been so cruelly snatched. But soon, he began to feel comfort from the leafy green branches, and even sighed softly when the gentle winds brought them close to his aching body.

The Waq-Waq remembered the days when he had had many friends around him. Little by little, even though he did not have his beautiful flower sprouting from his chest, he began to change his ways. Blanket-Ears helped the other Waq-Waqs return to the corner of the jungle, and the once lonely Waq-Waq was alone no more. That spring, a new flower sprouted from his heart.

After many years, the seafarer and the traveler returned to the jungle and saw the wonderful changes that had taken place. Some of the Waq-Waqs boarded his ship and returned to their island, and some decided to stay in the jungle. They all lived happily ever after, and the wicked witch was never seen again.

گربهٔ خودخواه

روزی بود روزگاری بود. زیر گنبد کبود دختری بود به نام زیباسته که خیلی مهربان
و خوشگل بود. ولی یک مشکل داشت. مشکلش آن بود که چیزی نداشت که با آن
پیشاب کند. زیباسته گربه ای تنبل و چاق و چله داشت که همیشه یا می خورد یا
می خوابید و دو تا چیز داشت. زیباسته به گربهٔ تنبلش خیلی مهربانی می کرد، و هر
وقت که می خواست پیشاب کند یکی از چیزهای گربه را قرض می گرفت. ولی گربه
خیلی خود خواه بود. گاهی زیباسته ساعت ها در انتظار می ماند، و گربه هر بار
پاداشی بیشتر و بهتر از او درخواست می کرد.

یک روز زیباسته با مادرش برای خرید به مرکز شهر رفت. ناگهان چندین سوارکار
با پرچم های رنگین به مرکز شهر رسیدند و اعلام کردند: "اندکی دیگر شاهزاده از
این جا گذر خواهد کرد. به دو کنار جادّه بروید و هنگام عبور کالسکه اش به او
تعظیم کنید."

شاهزاده بیشتر وقت در کاخ بود، و تنها کسانی را که می دید درباریان و پاسداران
کاخ بودند. به این دلیل، وقتی از کاخ بیرون می آمد خیلی علاقه داشت که دنیای
خارج از کاخ و مردم معمولی را ببیند.

وقتی که کالسکهٔ شاهزاده از جلو زیباسته و مادرش رد می شد، زیباسته از کنجکاوی
سرش را بالا برد تا به شاهزاده نگاهی بیندازد. درست در آن حالی که زیباسته سرش

را بالا برد تا شاهزاده را ببیند، شاهزاده هم از دریچهٔ کالسکه به سوی او نگاه کرد. شاهزاده صورت زیبای زیباسته را دید و یک دل نه صد دل عاشق او شد.

شاهزاده به رانندهٔ کالسکه دستور داد، "اسب ها را نگه دار." راننده افسار اسب های سفید زیبا را کشید و کالسکه درجا ایستاد. شاهزاده با خودش فکر کرد، "من نازنین ترین دختر این سرزمین را دیده ام، نازنین ترین دختری که امکان دارد در یک عمر دید. باید ببینم این دختر کیست."

زیباسته ترسید که چون سرش را بالا برده است، باعث خشم اطرافیان شاهزاده شده است. از ترس با مادرش با شتاب از آن جا دور شد و به خانه بر گشت. شاهزاده به اطرافیانش دستور داد تا زیباسته را پیدا کنند، ولی از او هیچ اثری نبود.

وقتی که شاهزاده به کاخ برگشت، به پدرش گفت، "من زیبا ترین دختر این سرزمین را دیده ام. ولی وقتی کالسکه را نگاه داشتم که او را پیدا کنم، دختر زیبا از نظر ناپدید شد." پادشاه به درباریان دستور داد، "دختر زیبا را پیدا کنید و به کاخ بیاورید، تا او را ببینم." درباریان به شهر رفتند، در هر خانه را زدند و از این و آن پرسش کردند که آیا آن دختر زیبا را می شناسند.

پس از اندک زمانی دختر زیبا را پیدا کردند. زیباسته وقتی که دید درباریان در خانه را می زنند از ترس به لرزه افتاد. درباریان او را آرام کردند، و گفتند، "شاهزاده عاشق شما شده است، و می خواهد با شما ازدواج کند." زیباسته نگران شد، چون خجالت می کشید به آن ها بگوید که چیزش را از گربه قرض می گیرد و گفت، "ما خانواده ای فقیر هستیم و من درخور شأن شاهزاده نیستم." درباریان جواب دادند، "این موضوع برای شاهزاده مهمّ نیست." زیباسته بهانه ای دیگر پیدا کرد و گفت، "مادر من سالخورده است و به کمک من احتیاج دارد." درباریان گفتند، "شاهزاده هر آن چه را که لازم باشد برای خانوادهٔ شما تعیین خواهد کرد."

زیباسته که دید چاره ای نیست به درباریان گفت، "من گربه ای ملوس دارم، و او را خیلی دوست می دارم. گربه همه جا با من است، و بدون او نمی دانم چه کنم." درباریان نمی دانستند چرا زیباسته این همه بهانه پیدا می کند. از ترس آن که اگر

زیباسته را به کاخ نیاورند پادشاه خشمگین خواهد شد، به او گفتند، "هیچ چیز نمی تواند تصمیم پادشاه را عوض کند. گربه را بگیرید و با ما به کاخ بیایید، چون که پادشاه و شاهزاده در انتظار شما هستند." زیباسته گربه اش را گرفت و با درباریان به کاخ رفت.

وقتی به کاخ رسیدند، پادشاه نگاهی به زیباستهٔ مهربان وخوشگل انداخت و از انتخاب شاهزاده خوشحال شد. پادشاه ازدواج شاهزاده را با زیباسته تأیید کرد و برای آن ها دعای خیر کرد. پادشاه به درباریان دستور داد جشن عروسی بزرگی را ترتیب دهند و مهمانانی زیاد را به جشن عروسی دعوت کنند.

گربهٔ خودخواه که زرق و برق کاخ پر نعمت را دید، با افاده خودش را خیلی بالا گرفت و به زیباسته گفت، "از این به بعد من پاداش هایی بیشتر و بهتر می خواهم، اگر نه چیزم را به قرض نخواهم داد." زیباستهٔ حیرت زده پرسید، "چه می خواهی؟" گربه با خودخواهی گفت، "من هم مثل تو بهترین غذاها را می خواهم." زیباسته قبول کرد. گربه با نخوت ادامه داد، "هر روز تو باید ساعت ها من را نوازش و آرایش کنی." زیباسته قبول کرد. گربه با تحقیر و ریشخند گفت، "هر روز باید من را بشویی و موهایم را شانه کنی. هر چند بار که موهایم خیلی بلند شد باید موهایم را کوتاه کنی تا راحت باشم."

زیباسته که می دانست شب عروسی به چیز گربه احتیاج دارد، به گربه گفت، "خیلی خوب هرچه را که بخواهی به تو می دهم، به این شرط که شب عروسی تا صبح مزاحم من و شاهزاده نشوی." گربه قبول کرد.

جشن عروسی بسیار زیبا بود. سفره ها پر از غذاهای خوشمزّه بودند و شیرینی های لذیذ. نوازندگان آهنگ هایی دل نواز نواختند و همه از خوشحالی تا سحر به رقص و پایکوبی در آمدند. مهمانان زیادی که آن جا بودند برای عروس و داماد آرزوی یک عمر خوشی و سلامتی کردند. ولی هیچ کس نمی دانست تا چه اندازه زیباسته نگران است چون می ترسید که گربهٔ خودخواه زیر قولش بزند.

سرانجام شاهزاده زیباسته را به حجله برد. گربه هم به دنبال نوعروس دوید. زیباسته گربه را به دست گرفت و موهایش را نوازش کرد، ولی گربهٔ خودخواه شروع کرد نق نق کردن، و در گوش زیباسته پچ پچ کرد و گفت، "من حاضر نیستم چیزم را تا صبح به تو قرض بدهم. همین حالا آن را به من بر گردان." زیباسته لرزید گربه را زمین گذاشت و به گریه افتاد.

شاهزاده اشک های او را دید و به او نزدیک شد تا او را آرام کند. شاهزادهٔ عاقل که دید گربه مزاحم زیباسته است، شمشیرش را از غلاف کشید و "گربه را در حجله کشت." بعد از آن زیباسته هیچ چیز کم نداشت. زیباسته و شاهزاده و بچّه هایشان سال ها با خوشی و سلامتی با هم زندگی کردند.

۲۴

چوپان و جادوگر

روزی بود روزگاری بود. زیر گنبد کبود جادوگری عاقل بود، که پسری با هوش داشت. روزی پسر جادوگر از او پرسید، "چرا بعضی زیاده گسارند، وبعضی نانی برای خوردن ندارند؟" جادوگر به پسرش گفت، "بیا با هم در اطراف شهر گردشی کنیم، تا تو جواب پرسشت را پیدا کنی."

با هم به کوهی در خارج از شهر رسیدند. جادوگر به پسرش گفت، "در بالای این کوه مرد پیری در خانه ای یک اطاقه زندگی می کند. در حیاط کوچک خانه اش یک درخت گردو هست و یک چاه آب. درخت گردوی روزی یک دانه گردو به بار می آورد، و مرد پیر غذایش یک گردو در روز است. من با جادو شاخه های درخت گردو را پر از گردو می کنم، وچاه را لبریز از آب. پس از آن من و تو با هم به دیدن او خواهیم رفت، تا با هم یکی دو تا گردو بخوریم و کمی آب بنوشیم."

جادوگر چوب دستی جادویش را بالا و پایین برد و زیر لب جادویی خواند، و به پسرش گفت، "درخت گردوی مرد پیر را آن قدر پر از گردو کردم که شاخه هایش خم شده اند و چاهش آن قدر پر از آب که قطره های آب از لبۀ چاه به حیاط می چکند."

درعین حالی که جادوگر و پسرش از کوه بالا می رفتند. مرد پیر دید که ناگهان درخت گردو پر برکت و پر از گردو شده است. گردوها را چید و در صندوقی در اطاقش گذاشت. همچنین دید که چاه خانه اش لبریز از آب است. سطلی را هم پر از آب کرد و در اطاقش پنهان کرد.

جادوگر و پسرش به خانهٔ مرد پیر رسیدند و در زدند. مرد پیر در خانه را باز کرد، نیمه باز گذاشت و با شکّ و تردید به آن ها نگاه کرد. جادوگر به مرد پیر گفت، "ما ساعت ها در این گرما راه رفته ایم تا به بالای این کوه برسیم. من و پسر جوانم خیلی تشنه ایم. آیا می توانید جرعهٔ آبی به ما بدهید تا بنوشیم؟" مرد پیر جواب داد، "من مردی پیر و فقیرم. کاش آبی یا غذایی داشتم تا از شما پذیرایی کنم." پس از آن که جادوگر و پسرش آن جا را ترک کردند، مرد پیر به اطاقش بر گشت و دید که موشی مشغول جویدن یکی از گردوهاست.

جادوگر و پسرش از کوه پایین رفتند و به دشت سبزی رسیدند، که رودی از میان آن رد می شد. در آن جا چوپانی را دیدند که گلّه بزرگی از گوسفندان داشت. جادوگر چوبدستی جادویش را بالا و پایین برد و جادویی خواند. باد تندی وزید وگوسفندان چوپان هر یک به طرفی دیگر پراکنده شدند.

چوپان سعی کرد نگذارد گوسفندانش فرار کنند. می دانست که در جنگل نزدیک آن دشت گرگ ها زوزه می کشند، و در کوه های طرف دیگر بزهای کوهی با شاخ های تیزشان به دیدارگران شاخ می زنند. و همچنین می دانست که جریان آب رودخانه آن قدر قویست که می تواند گوسفندان را با خود ببرد. مدّتی زیاد به دنبال گوسفندان دوید تا آن ها را جمع کند، ولی فقط چند تا از آن ها را پیدا کرد. سر انجام چوپان خسته در کنار رودخانه نشست و آبی نوشید.

جادوگر و پسرش به آن جا نزدیک شدند. تا چوپان آن ها را دید با خوشحالی گفت، "دوستان بیایید با هم غذایی بخوریم. مهمان من باشید، چون وقتی غذایمان را با هم قسمت کنیم، از گرسنگی اثری نمی ماند." چوپان بقچهٔ غذایش را باز کرد و سفره ای انداخت. از داخل بقچه همهٔ نان های تنک را در آورد و روی سفره گذاشت. مقدار کمی پنیر گوسفند را هم که داشت روی سفره گذاشت. از چند گوسفندی که برایش مانده بودند شیر گرفت و به مهمانانش داد.

اندکی بعد چند نفر از افراد ده نزدیک از آن جا رد می شدند. آن ها خسته و گرسنه به نظر می رسیدند. چوپان آن ها را هم به نهار دعوت کرد. به آن ها گفت، "وقتی

غذایمان را با هم قسمت کنیم، از گرسنگی اثری نمی‌ماند." باز جادوگر جادویی کرد، سفره پر از نان و پنیر شد، و همه سیر شدند.

جادوگر و پسرش از چوپان سپاسگزاری کردند و با او خدا حافظی کردند. وقتی از چوپان دور شدند، جادوگر چوبدستی جادویش را بالا و پایین برد و جادویی خواند. همهٔ گوسفندان از هر گوشه به چوپان باز گشتند. سگی با وفا هم به گله پیوست و از آن به بعد از گوسفندان نگهبانی کرد.

مرد پیر روزی یک گردو خورد، و سفرهٔ چوپان همیشه پر از نعمت بود. پسر جادوگر هم درسی آموخت.

سفری به سرزمین تاریکی

روزی بود روزگاری بود. زیر گنبد کبود جوانی بود بسیار دلیر و زورمند. او و گروهی
از دوستانش تصمیم گرفتند به سرزمین تاریکی سفر کنند. مرد جوان پدر پیری داشت
که خیلی عاقل بود، ولی لاغر و ضعیف بود، وحتّی به سختی می توانست راه برود.
پدر پیر در بیشتر ساعت های روز، یا کتاب می خواند، یا با پیرمردان دیگر محلّه
صحبت می کرد، و خودش را سرگرم می کرد. او در روزهای جوانی مردی خوش قامت
و سینه ستبر بود، و موهای سرش پر و سیاه و پر موج بود. در جوانی به همه جای دنیا
سفر کرده بود، و به این دلیل جهان دیده ای خیلی عاقل و پرتجربه بود.

وقتی پدر مرد جوان برنامهٔ سفر او را به سرزمین تاریکی شنید، به او هشیار داد،
"سفری را که در سر داری سفریست فریب آمیز و پرخطر. به راه نمایی کار آزموده
ای نیاز داری که به کمک او به آن جا سفر کنی و به سلامت بر گردی." مرد جوان به
پدرش گفت، "وقتی از این سفر بر گردم، مثل شما عاقل و با تجربه خواهم شد. ولی
حرف شما صحیح است، اگر وضعی فریب آمیز در راه باشد که ما با آن آشنا نباشیم،
ممکن است جانمان در خطر بیفتد." پدرش به او گفت، "من را در در کالسکه ات
پنهان کن و با خود به سفر ببر، و گاه گاهی در طول سفر با من مشورت کن."

مرد جوان و گروه دوستانش خود را برای سفر آماده کردند. توشه های کافی آماده
کردند، بارها را بستند و بسته ها و صندوق ها را در کالسکه هایشان گذاشتند. مرد
جوان پدرش را در بین بار وبندیل ها در کالسکه اش پنهان کرد. گروه جوانان بر

کالسکه ها سوار شدند، و اسب های خوب و پرتوانشان کالسکه ها را با سرعت به سوی سرزمین تاریکی پیش بردند.

وقتی به سرزمین تاریکی نزدیک شدند، پدر پیر با صدایی خفیف به پسرش گفت، "به دوستانت بگو نعل اسب ها را از پای اسب ها در آورند. این سرزمین چون آهن ربایی بزرگ است. اگر نعل اسب ها را در نیاورید پای های اسب ها آن چنان به زمین خواهند چسبید که ادامهٔ سفر غیر ممکن خواهد شد." مرد جوان، بدون آنکه نامی از پدرش ببرد، این پیام را به دوستانش رسانید.

چندی از جوانان زود دست به کار شدند و نعل اسب ها را در آوردند. ولی گروهی به این پیشنهاد خندیدند و با تمسخر این اندیشه را کنار گذاشتند. مرد جوان، بدون آن که آشکار کند که پدر جهان دیده اش با اوست، کوشش کرد آن ها را راضی کند. به آن ها گفت که مردان جهان دیده به او گوشزد کرده اند که بین زمین معمولی، و زمینی که نیروهایی عمیق در درون دارد، تفاوتی زیاد هست.

گروه مسافران به راه ادامه دادند. روزها تاریک تر و تاریک تر شدند، و نیروی آهن ربایی زمین قوی تر و قوی تر. دوستانی که نعل اسب ها را در آورده بودند به آسانی به راه ادامه دادند. آن ها که سرسخت بودند و نعل اسب ها را در نیاورده بودند، اسب هایشان آهسته تر و آهسته تر راه رفتند و عاقبت در جا ماندند.

جوانان به راهی پر از سنگ رسیدند. پدر پیر با صدایی سکوت آمیز به پسرش گفت، "به دوستانت بگو که چند تا از این سنگ ها را بر دارند و روی کالسکه هایشان بار کنند. آنان که خیلی کم بار کنند پشیمان خواهند شد، و آنان که خیلی زیاد بار کنند پشیمان خواهند شد." مرد جوان پند پدرش را برای دوستانش باز گو کرد.

چندی به این حرف ها خندیدند و هیچ سنگی بر نداشتند وچندی سنگ هایی زیاد بار کردند. آن ها که میانه رو بودند چندین سنگ را بر داشتند و در کالسکه هایشان گذاشتند.

آن ها که هیچ سنگی بر نداشتند، جلو تر از همه پیش رفتند. کسانی که به خاطر سنگ های زیاد بار اسب هایشان خیلی سنگین شده بود، نتوانستند به راهشان ادامه

دهند و عقب ماندند. آنان که با میانه روی سنگ هایی چند بار کرده بودند با آرامی و پیوستگی به راهشان ادامه دادند.

به جنگلی پر از درخت رسیدند. پدر پیر باز با صدایی سکوت آمیز به پسرش گفت، "به دوستانت بگو خیلی با احتیاط از این جنگل گذر کنند. در شاخه های بعضی از این درخت ها مارهایی زهرین جا کرده اند، و بر شاخه های درختان دیگر میوه هایی مغذّی آویزانند. به آن ها بگو از مارها پرهیز کنند و میوه های خوب را بچینند و جمع کنند، چون سفر دراز است و توشه ها در حال خالی شدن. به آن ها بگو در انتخاب درختان هشیار باشند، چون که مارهای فریب کار گاهی روی درختان پر میوه می نشینند."

طبق معمول چندی به این پند عاقلانهٔ پدر پیر توجّهی نکردند. آن ها که بی صبر و آزمند بودند، بدون توجّه از درختان بالا رفتند و به جای میوه با مارهایی سهمناک رو به رو شدند. چندی مسافر تنبل، به خیال آن که توشهٔ راهشان کافیست، به خود زحمتی ندادند و هیچ میوه ای نچیدند. ولی آن ها که عاقل و صبور بودند با دقّت درختان خوب را پیدا کردند و از آن ها میوه چیدند، و با توشه ای کافی به راهشان ادامه دادند.

روزی که تاریکی به عمقی بی مانند رسیده بود، و چشم هیچ کس راهی را نمی دید، پدر پیر به پسرش گفت، "به دوستانت بگو که به عمق تاریکی رسیده اند. برای پیدا کردن راه بازگشت نمی توانند چشم هایشان را به کار ببرند. به آن ها بگو به هر صدایی، هر چند که خفیف باشد، گوش کنند. همچنین به آن ها بگو هر رایحه ای را با هشیاری بو کنند. و مهم ترین امر آنست که نگذارند هیچ چیز آن ها را از ادامهٔ راه بترساند."

چندی که ترس بر آن ها چیره شده بود، به خیال های بد و تیره رسیدند و راهشان را گم کردند. آنان که نه به رایحه ای توجّه کردند و نه به صدایی، به بیراهه رفتند. آن ها که با هشیاری به اطرافشان توجّه کردند، بدون ترس به راهشان ادامه دادند. جوان دلیر و دوستان باقی مانده اش، به کمک پدر پیرش، کم کم از سرزمین تاریکی بیرون آمدند، به نور روز رسیدند، و سر انجام به خانه بر گشتند.

آنان که از سرزمین تاریکی سنگ هایی چند بار کرده بودند، به سنگ ها نگاه انداختند. با شگفتی دریافتند که این سنگ ها کم یاب ترین و پر ارزش ترین سنگ های الماسند. سنگ ها را فروختند و پرمال و ثروت شدند. مهم تر از همه چیز آن بود که، جوانانی که به سرزمین تاریکی سفر کرده بودند و به سلامت باز گشته بودند، عاقل تر شده بودند، و در طریق زندگی پر تجربه تر. در طول زمان کودکانشان بزرگ شدند, و چندی از آن ها فرزندان جوانشان را، از درون کالسکه ها، در سرزمین تاریکی راهنمایی کردند.

فاطمه نساء

روزی بود روزگاری بود. زیر گنبد کبود، زن گازری بود که در دهی نزدیک رودخانه ای زندگی می کرد. گازر خری وفادار داشت و دو بچّه ، دختری زیبا به نام فاطمه نساء و پسری خوش رفتار به نام فیصل که کچل بود. فاطمه نساء و فیصل یک دیگر را خیلی دوست می داشتند.

یک روز گازر بقچه ای پر از لباس را روی خرش گذاشت و با دخترش فاطمه نساء به کنار رودخانه رفت تا لباس ها را بشوید. بر گردن خر زنگله ای خوش نوا آویزان بود و در طول راه پیوسته جلنگ جلنگ می کرد. خر در دلش می گفت:

"جلنگ جلنگ می رویم
راه پر سنگ می رویم
با فاطمه نساء می دویم "

وقتی گازر به رودخانه رسید، نگاه کرد تا جایی مناسب برای لباس شویی پیدا کند. در عین حال دخترش به این بر و آن بر رفت تا بازی کند. گازر دخترش را صدا زد، ولی از فاطمه نساء جوابی نشنید. به دور و برش نگاه کرد تا ببیند دخترش کجاست، ولی از فاطمه نساء خبری نبود.

خر زنگله به گردن که دید فاطمه نساء گم شده است، چهار نعل به این بر و آن بر دوید و گفت:

"جلنگ جلنگ فاطمه نساء را بردند
بس نبود یونجهٔ ما را خوردند"

گازر نگران از آن که فاطمه نساء گم شده است، خر را صدا زد، سوار خر شد و به خانه برگشت. با گریه به پسرش گفت "فیصل جان عزیزم، خواهرت گم شده است." فیصل مادر بی چاره اش را آرام کرد و به او گفت، "من گنجشکی را می شناسم که از کودکی با او دوست بوده ام. به کمک او فاطمه نساء را پیدا خواهم کرد."

فیصل دوید تا به لانهٔ گنجشک رسید، و فریاد کشید "گنجشک عزیز عاقل خواهرم گم شده است. به من کمک کن تا او را پیدا کنم." گنجشک جواب داد "اگر غذایت را با من قسمت کنی، به تو کمک می کنم." فیصل گفت "من چند چغندر قند را تمام شب روی منقل گذاشته ام. این لبوهای شیرین و خوش مزّه را با تو قسمت می کنم."

فیصل سفره را پهن کرد و لبو را روی آن گذاشت، و آن دو شروع کردند به خوردن. فیصل کچل لف لف تکّه های بزرگ لبو را خورد، و گنجشک بی چاره فرصت نمی کرد چنگ خود را به لبو بزند. گنجشک گله کرد:

" لفّی تو و من چنگی کم
با لفّ تو چون سیر شوم"

فیصل معذرت خواست و تکّهٔ بزرگی از لبو را پیش گنجشک گذاشت.

وقتی که گنجشک سیر شد فیصل از او پرسید "چه گونه فاطمه نساء را پیدا کنیم؟" گنجشک جواب داد "من در هوا پرواز می کنم، و از مرغان دیگر پرسش می کنم، تا ببینم فاطمه نساء را به کجا برده اند. وقتی او را پیدا کردم، باز خواهم گشت و راه را به تو نشان خواهم داد."

گنجشک مدّتی پرواز کرد و برگشت و به فیصل گفت، "خواهر تو در برج و باروی غول هاست. در این برج و بارو غولی جوان زندگی می کند که هنوز شاخ و دم در نیاورده است. غول جوان بی شاخ و دم عاشق فاطمه نساء شده است، و می خواهد بدون رضایت فاطمه نساء با او عروسی کند."

فیصل نگران شد. اندیشهٔ این که غولی با خواهرش عروسی کند و خواهرزاده هایش شاخ و دم داشته باشند او را ترساند. با دلهره از گنجشک پرسید "برج و باروی غول ها کجاست؟" گنجشک جواب داد، "من در هوا پرواز می کنم و راه را به تو نشان می دهم. تو روی خرت سوار شو و به دنبال من بیا."

فیصل سوار خر زنگله دارش شد و با شتاب به راه افتاد. خر فریاد کشید:

"جلنگ جلنگ فاطمه را به زور بردند
جلنگ جلنگ به راه دور بردند
جلنگ جلنگ به جنگ غول می رویم
با فاطمه نساء زدست غول می رهیم"

گنجشک خیلی بالا در هوا پرواز می کرد، و فیصل به دنبال او برای مدّت زیادی خرش را راند. سرانجام گنجشک در کنار رود خانه ای پایین آمد و گفت، "از هوا می توانم برج و بارو را ببینم. بیا تا مدّتی در این جا استراحت کنیم و غذایی بخوریم." فیصل سفره را پهن کرد و لبویش را روی آن گذاشت. دو باره فیصل کچل شروع کرد لف لف خوردن. گنجشک که نمی توانست چنگ خودش را به لبو بزند گله کرد:

" لقّی تو و من چنگی کم
با لفّ تو چون سیر شوم"

خر هم که خیلی خسته و گرسنه بود وارد بحث شد:

" لقّی تو و من خسته و بی جو
من چون بزنم پای به دو"

فیصل تکهٔ بزرگی از لبو را پیش گنجشک گذاشت، و کیسهٔ جو را از پشت خر پایین آورد و جلو او گذاشت تا بخورد.

وقتی همه سیر شدند، آب خوردند و استراحت کردند، فیصل از گنجشک پرسید، "چه گونه می توانم به برج و بارو وارد شوم، تا خواهرم را از چنگ این غول بی شاخ و دم آزاد کنم؟" گنجشک جواب داد، "من راه ورود به برج و بارو را به تو نشان خواهم داد، ولی قبل از آن باید طلسم جادو را پیدا کنیم."

فیصل پرسید، "کدام طلسم؟" گنجشک جواب داد، "در دوران قدیم هنرمندی پاکدل و عاقل طلسمی کوچک ساخت و روی آن چهل دعا حکّ کرد. اگرکسی در مقابل غولی طلسم را به دست بگیرد و حتّی یک دعا از آن را بخواند، جادوی طلسم رها می شود، و باعث می شود که غول ناتوان بشود و به زمین بیفتد."

فیصل پرسید، "طلسم جادو کجاست؟" گنجشک نوکی به لبو زد و گفت، "غول ها آن قدر از این طلسم وحشت داشتند که به کمک ساحره ای کژ رفتار آن را در غاری در اوج کوهی بلند پنهان کردند. پس از آن غول ها را در غار با سنگی خیلی بزرگ بستند. ولی روزنه ای مستور هست که از آن می توانم به غار وارد شوم و طلسم را برایت بیاورم."

آفتاب داشت به مغرب می نشست و هوا داشت تاریک می شد. فیصل که خسته و خواب آلود بود گفت، "فردا صبح زود به راهمان ادامه خواهیم داد." هر یک از آن سه فرد گوشهٔ راحتی را پیدا کرد تا شب را در آن جا به سر برد. هنگام سحر گنجشک به هوا پرید و به اوج کوه بلند رسید. از روزنهٔ مستور وارد غار شد. طلسم را به چَنگ گرفت و به فیصل باز گشت.

وقتی که آفتاب همه جا را روشن کرد، غول ها مثل هر روز از برج و بارو بیرون رفتند. تا که غول ها رفتند گنجشک از راهی مخفی وارد برج و بارو شد و فیصل و خرش هم به دنبال او روان شدند. فیصل دستش را در جیبش روی طلسم جادو گذاشت و ترسش ریخت. آن ها با شتاب در خانهٔ غول ها به جستجو پرداختند تا خواهر گم شدهٔ فیصل را پیدا کنند.

پس از مدّتی جستجو، در زیرزمینی خانه به اطاقی تاریک رسیدند، که پنجره ای آهنین و دری بزرگ و آهنین داشت. دربسته بود و قفلی بزرگ رویش بود. فیصل از پنجره نگاه کرد و فاطمه نساء و چندین زندانی بیچارهٔ دیگر را در آن اطاق دید. فیصل خوشحال از دیدن خواهرش فریاد کشید، "آمده ام تا تو را آزاد کنم." فاطمه نساء جواب داد، "این غول ها خیلی ستم کار و خطرناکند. اگر تو را بگیرند، برای همیشه در این جا زندانی خواهند کرد." فیصل فاطمه نساء را آرام کرد و به او گفت، "نگران نباش. طلسمی جادویی در جیب دارم که غول ها را ضعیف و ناتوان می کند."

در عین حال، گنجشک عاقل به این طرف و آن طرف و به چپ و راست و بالا و پایین پرید و ترکی در دیوار دید. به سوی ترک پرید و کلید قفل را در آن جا پیدا کرد. ولی کلید برای گنجشک کوچک سنگین بود. فیصل روی خر ایستاد و دستش به کلید رسید. کلید را برداشت و از خر پایین پرید. قفل را باز کرد و فاطمه نساء وهمهٔ زندانی ها را آزاد کرد.

همه با شتاب از برج و بارو بیرون دویدند. ولی تا همه از برج و بارو بیرون آمدند، یکی از بزرگ ترین و زشت ترین غول ها آن ها را در حال فرار دید. غول ها غریوان به آن جا نزدیک شدند و با صدایی گوش خراش فریاد زدند:

"فریاد

ای داد بی دا

بوی آدمی زاد میاد"

فیصل طلسم را از جیبش در آورد، با دستی توانا آن را مقابل غول عظیم الجثّه و زشت رو گرفت ویک دعای طلسم را با صدای بلند خواند. غول بزرگ به لرزه افتاد، رنگ از صورت زشتش پرید. چشم چپ تهوّع انگیزش بسته شد، و با تاپ لرزنده ای به زمین افتاد. غول های دیگر نزدیک شدند تا ببینند چه بلایی به سر غول زشت عظیم الجثّه آمده است. آن ها هم به همان سرنوشت گرفتار شدند. چند غول دیگر که این ماجرا را از دور دیدند، آن قدر به ترس افتادند که برگشتند و به سر زمینی دور دست فرار کردند. حتّی غول جوان بی شاخ و دم هم که عاشق فاطمه نساء شده بود و می خواست با او ازدواج کند از طلسم ترسید، دست از عاشقی بر داشت و فرار کرد.

گنجشک راه باز گشت را به همه نشان داد. همه به خانه هایشان و عزیزانشان رسیدند، وغول ها دیگر هیچ وقت مزاحم آن ها نشدند. پس از آن ، وقتی که فاطمه نساء با مادرش به رودخانه می رفت هرگز از او دور نشد. همچنین دیگر هیچ کس به فیصل نگفت کچل، چون همیشه با سخاوت غذایش را با گنجشک و دیگران قسمت می کرد، و به اندازهٔ کافی به خرش جو و یونجه می داد.

بنّای شادمان

روزی بود روزگاری بود. زیر گنبد کبود، مرد جوان پرتوان و شادمانی بود، که کارش بنّایی بود. در عین حالی که سخت کار می کرد، آواز می خواند و همیشه لبخند می زد. رفتار او کارگرهای دیگر را هم که دور و بر او بودند خوشحال می کرد.

یک روز دو تاجر از مکان کار او می گذشتند. این دو تاجر همیشه با هم جرّ و بحث می کردند و در هر مورد شرط می بستند. هر یک می خواست نقطه نظر خودش را به دیگری ثابت کند. در حالی که از مکان کار بنّای شادمان رد می شدند، تاجر جوان به تاجر سالخورده گفت، "من فکر می کنم مردمانی چون او از روز تولّد خوشحالند." تاجر سالخورده گفت، "نه، روش زندگی آن ها و مردم دور و برشان باعث شادمانی آن ها هستند." با هم جرّ و بحث را ادامه دادند و برای اثبات نظرشان شرط بندی کردند.

تاجر سالخورده، که عقیده داشت می توان شادمانی را به وجود آورد، گفت، "من با تو شرط می بندم که می توانم این بنّا را آن قدر غمگین و جدا افتاده کنم که از کارش متنفّر بشود و به کندی کار کند. و شرط می بندم که پس از آن که او را از آن حالا هم شادمان تر کنم." تاجر جوان که عقیده داشت مردم خوشحال به دنیا می آیند، گفت، "من فکر می کنم که چنین کاری غیر ممکن است. من شرط می بندم که تو نخواهی توانست چنین کاری بکنی." آن دو برای ده سکّهٔ طلا شرط بستند و به هم دست دادند.

تاجر سالخورده به یکی از کمک کارانش گفت که به محلّ کار وزندگی بنّای جوان برود و ببیند روش زندگی او چه گونه است. کمک کار تاجر که مردی با هوش و آگاه بود، همسایه های بنّا را پیدا کرد و با آن ها حرف زد و خیلی چیزها پرسید. به تاجر برگشت و به این گونه گزارش داد، "بنّا زنی بسیار زیبا دارد، که خیلی زیاد دوستش دارد. هر روز که بنّا از کار بر می گردد، زنش برای او آب گرم می کند تا خودش را بشوید. برایش لباس های تمیز می آورد تا لباس هایش را عوض کند، وبرایش خوراک های خوش مزّه می آورد که در عرض روز پخته است. زنش آرام بخش است و پر از محبّت، و به شوهرش مهربانی زیادی نشان می دهد. بنّای جوان هم زنش را همچنان دوست می دارد و محبّتش را جبران می کند. برایش هدیه می آورد، و کوشش می کند همیشه او را شادمان نگاه دارد. برای زنش آواز می خواند، و برایش داستان های خنده دار تعریف می کند. خانهٔ آن ها پر از خنده و شادی است. آن ها دوستان خوبی هم دارند و گاه گاهی به دیدن یک دیگر می روند."

تاجر سالخورده نقشه ای کشید. او یکی از خادمانش را به محلّ کار بنّا فرستاد، تا با او آشنا و دوست بشود. او همچنین زنی را که در خانه اش خدمتکار بود به محلّ زندگی بنّا و زنش فرستاد تا با زن بنّا آشنا و دوست شود.

پس از آن که خادم با بنّای جوان دوست شد، و اعتماد او را به دست آورد، به او گفت، "دوست عزیزم خبری ناخوش آیند برای تو دارم. وقتی که تو سر کار هستی و این جا سخت مشغول کاری زن تو را با مردی دیگر دیده اند." زن خدمتکار هم، که با زن بنّا دوست شده بود، به او گفت، "وقتی که تو در خانه غذا می پزی و برای شوهرت آب گرم می کنی، بارها شوهرت کار را کنار می گذارد و با زنی دیگر خوش گذرانی می کند."

چند روز گذشت و بنّا و زنش به این حرف ها اعتنایی نکردند. ولی در روزهای بعد، دو خدمتکار تاجر سالخورده بیشتر و بیشتر برای بنّا و زنش دروغ بافتند. شکّ و تردید کم کم در دل بنّا رخنه کرد. شب ها نمی توانست به خواب برود. نمی توانست به راحتی غذا بخورد. سر کار حواسش جمع نبود. روز به روز غمگین تر و غمگین تر شد. زنش هم آن قدر غمگین و نگران شده بود که میل غذا پختن نداشت. برای شوهرش آب گرم نمی کرد و حتّی صبر و حوصله نداشت با شوهرش حرف بزند.

تاجر سالخورده دوست جوانش را خواند تا به او نشان بدهد، بنّای جوان تا چه اندازه غمگین شده و چه قدر به کندی کار می کند. تاجر جوان باور نمی توانست کند که بنّای بی چاره به چه روزی افتاده است، و خیلی دلش به حال او سوخت. به تاجر سالخورده التماس کرد که وضع بنّای غمگین را عوض کند. تاجر سالخورده گفت، "آن چنان که شرط بستم می توانم او را از غم رها کنم، و حتّی از گذشته هم او را شادمان تر کنم." تاجر سالخورده به خدمتکارانش گفت که به بنّا و زنش بروند و آن ها را دو باره به هم نزدیک کنند و بین آن ها هماهنگی به وجود آورند.

خادم تاجر به بنّا رفت و فراوان پوزش خواست و تمنّای بخشش کرد، "مرا ببخش چون اشتباهاً خیال کردم زنی دیگر زن تو است. وقتی تو را به این اندازه غمگین دیدم به خودم گفتم شاید اشتباه کرده باشم. از همسایه هایتان پرس و جو کردم وهمه یک صدا گفتند زن تو زنی پاکدامن و مهربان است، که فوق العاده به شوهرش وفادار است، و او را دوست می دارد."

زن خدمتکار تاجر هم به دیدن زن بنّا رفت و زیاد عذر خواهی کرد و گفت، "مرا ببخش چون اشتباهاً خیال کردم مردی دیگر شوهر تو است. از آن که بدون فکر به نتیجه های غلط رسیدم بی اندازه شرمنده ام. از این و آن پرس و جو کردم و همه گفتند شوهر تو مردی با وفا و خوش رفتار است که از ته قلب زنش را دوست می دارد."

آن شب، وقتی که بنّای جوان به خانه برگشت، برای زنش هدیه ای آورد، برای او آواز خواند وقصّه های خنده دار تعریف کرد. زنش برای او آب گرم آماده کرده بود. پس از شست و شو برای او لباس های تمیز آورد. سفره را چید و برای شوهرش خوراک های خوش طعم و خوش بو آورد. بنّا و زنش خوشحال از آن که شکّ و تردیدیشان از یک دیگر بی اساس بوده است، غم را از دل زدودند و باز به یک دیگر پیوستند. بار دیگر بنّای جوان شادمان و پر امید شد، و در سر کار پر از توان کار می کرد و همه را خوشحال می کرد. زن بنّا حتّی بیش از گذشته به شوهرش مهربانی کرد و محبّت ورزید.

تاجر جوان ده سکّهٔ طلا به تاجر سالخورده داد و گفت، "تو شرط را بردی". تاجر سالخورده تصمیم گرفت هدیه ای به بنّا و زنش بدهد و آن ها را حتّی خوشحال تر کند. در منطقه ای آبرومند از شهر خانه ای گران قیمت خرید که خیلی راحت و زیبا بود. با کمک خادمانش آن خانه را با قیمتی خیلی کم تر به بنّا فروخت. بنّا و زنش سال های سال با خوشی در آن خانه زندگی کردند، و چندین بچّهٔ شادمان را با هم بزرگ کردند.

۲۸

دو دوست و چوب دستی جادو

روزی بود روزگاری بود. زیر گنبد کبود دو پسر جوان بودند که با هم دوستانی صمیمی بودند. یکی به نام گرشاسب که خیلی پرتوان بود و کنجکاو و دیگری به نام برزوی که خیلی باهوش بود و پردانش و چندین زبان می دانست. آن دو آن چنان یک دیگر را خوب می شناختند که اگر یکی از آن ها کمانی می کشید، دیگری می دانست تیر به کجا خواهد نشست.

وقتی بزرگ تر شدند، یک روز گرشاسب به برزوی گفت، "بیا به دور دنیا سفر کنیم و تا آنجا که ممکن است شهرهای زیادی را ببینیم." برزوی موافقت کرد. آن دو توشهٔ راهشان را آماده کردند و بی ترس و دلهره برای دیدن دنیا به راه افتادند.

اوّل به شهری در کنار دریا رسیدند. در آن جا ماهی گیرانی را دیدند، که با قایق های بزرگ و تورهای بزرگشان ماهی می گرفتند. چندی از ماهی گیران با ماهی های فراوان از دریا برمی گشتند و چندی با کمی. برزوی به گرشاسب گفت، "ماهی گیر نه می تواند خیلی نزدیک به ساحل دریا ماهی بگیرد، نه خیلی دور از ساحل."

در ادامهٔ سفرشان به شهری در اوج سلسله کوه های بلند رسیدند. در آن جا سوارکارانی را دیدند که با مهارت اسب های بزرگ و زیبایشان را در جاده های پر پیچ و خم کوه ها می راندند. سوارکاران گاهی با هم بازی هایی شگفت انگیز می کردند وهر سوار کار با دیگری رقابت می کرد تا زبردستی خودش را نشان دهد. گروهی بازی

ها را می بردند، و گروهی می باختند. گرشاسب به برزوی گفت، " سوارکار پیروز با اسبش یکیست."

گرشاسب و برزوی به راهشان ادامه دادند و به شهری در کنار رودخانه ای رسیدند. در آن جا مردمانی نجیب و خوش رفتار را دیدند که در پخت و پز زبانزد اقوام دیگر بودند. درآن شهر خوش خوراک ترین غذا های ماهی و خوش عطر ترین شیرینی های خوش مزه را خوردند. برزوی گفت، "غذای آشپزهای ماهر پر از عطر دل انگیز است، ولی سفرهٔ مادر پر از عطر محبّت است."

به شهری در کوه های دوردست رسیدند. در آن جا هر یک از خانه ها در دل کوه حفر شده بود. در شب در هر خانه چراغی سوسو می زد و در آسمان ستاره ها در گلشن آسمان همچون پولک هایی سیمین می درخشیدند. گرشاسب گفت، "خدا عالم را آفرید و مردم شهرها را." هنگام سحر که ستاره ها به تدریج در آسمان محو می شدند از آن شهر بیرون آمدند.

گرشاسب و برزوی به سفرشان ادامه دادند، و به شهری رسیدند که پر از درختان زیبا و گل های خوش رنگ بود و مجسّمه های زیبا و ظریف. ساختمان های شهر هریک اثری هنری بود. در میان میدان مرکز شهر مجسّمه ای بزرگ و پرشکوه بود، که دلاوری را نشان می داد، که بر اسبی سوار بود. برزوی گفت، "دلاوری چون این پدر همهٔ مردم است."

سرانجام به خرابه های شهری باستانی رسیدند. قسمتی از ساختمان های شهر همان گونه زیبا و دست نخورده از دوران باستانی باقی مانده بودند. همهٔ ساختمان ها و دیوار های شهر از سنگ های بزرگ ساخته شده بودند. روی چندی از دیوارها نوشته هایی از دوران قدیم حکّ شده بودند.

به راهروی باریک رسیدند که به ندرت کسی در آن راه می رفت. وارد راهرو شدند و مدّتی راه رفتند تا به حیاطی تاریک رسیدند. در گرداگرد حیاط دیوارهای سنگی بلندی دیده می شدند، و در میان حیاط مجسمهٔ بزرگ یک گاو بود. مجسّمهٔ گاو روی پایه ای سنگی قرار داشت. بر روی پایهٔ مجسّمه نوشته ای به زبانی باستانی دیده می شد. برزوی نوشته را ترجمه کرد:

"سه بار ار مهر بر گاو تابید
یکی بسته دری را باز یابید"

دیوارهای اطراف حیاط آن قدر بلند بودند که به ندرت امکان داشت اشعهٔ آفتاب به مجسّمهٔ گاو بتابند. گرشاسب متوجّه شد که در دیوار پشت سر او روزنه ای گرد بود که از آن شعاعی از آفتاب به حیاط رخنه می کرد، و نقطه ای روشن روی دیوار مقابل می انداخت. آن دو مدّتی ایستادند و به نقطهٔ روشن نگاه کردند. هر چه وقت می گذشت و آفتاب در آسمان می گشت، نقطهٔ روشن در روی دیوار به تدریج بالاتر می رفت. و هر چه وقت می گذشت نقطه روشن به مجسّمهٔ گاو نزدیک تر می شد. سرانجام نقطهٔ روشن به صورت دایره ای کوچک و نورانی روی شاخ مجسّمهٔ گاو افتاد. گرشاسب شاخ مجسّمهٔ گاو را به دست گرفت، با آن بازی کرد و دید که می توان با زور آن را به جا جا کرد.

گرشاسب به برزوی رو کرد و با شور و هیجان گفت، "معنی سه بار آن است که باید شاخ گاو را سه بار در سه جهت حرکت دهیم." گرشاسب شاخ گاو را گرفت و با تمام توان به سوی آسمان بالا برد. صدایی شنیده شد که حاکی از لغزیدن تخته سنگی بزرگی بود روی سنگی دیگر. سپس گرشاسب شاخ را گرفت و با تمام نیرو پایین آورد، گفتی آن را به عمق دریا می رساند. این بار صدای لغزش تخته سنگ خفیف تر بود. گرشاسب برای بار سوّم شاخ را گرفت و با تمام قدرت به جای اوّلش برگرداند، مثل آن که هیچ چیز اتّفاق نیفتاده بود. ولی آن ها با تعجّب متوجّه شدند که در دیوار پشت سرشان دری بزرگ و سنگی باز شد، و راهروی تاریک را هویدا کرد.

بدون ترس و با احتیاط وارد راهرو شدند و زود چشم هایشان به تاریکی عادت کرد، به همان گونه که چشم به تاریکی شب عادت می کند. از راهرو به اطاقی کوچک و تاریک رسیدند. در میان اطاق سکویی بود. به سکو نزدیک شدند، و روی آن چوبدستی ای را دیدند. برزوی چوبدستی را برداشت، آن دو دوست از تاریکی بیرون آمدند و به حیاط برگشتند.

برزوی در نور حیاط به چوبدستی نگاه کرد و دید که نوشته ای به زبانی باستانی روی آن حکّ شده است. نوشته به این معنی بود:

"اگر نیکی کنی مهر و محبّت

ببارد زاسمان باران رحمت"

آفتاب داشت به مغرب می نشست، و باد سرد پائیز به تندی می وزید. نور روز داشت
کم کم به تاریکی تبدیل می شد و اوّلین ستاره های شب در آسمان کبود سو سو می
زدند. برزوی و گرشاسب ویرانه های باستانی را ترک کردند و پرسان پرسان به کاروان
سرایی رسیدند، تا شب را در آن جا سر کنند.

صبح روز بعد به راه افتادند و در نیمهٔ روز به شهری دیگر رسیدند. در دروازهٔ شهر
مرد پیری را دیدند که تشنه بود و عاجزانه درخواست آب می کرد. گرشاسب قمقمه
اش را باز کرد و کاسهٔ مرد پیر را پر از آب کرد. مرد پیر آب را نوشید، و از آن ها
پرسید، "چه امری شما را به این شهر آورده است؟" آن ها جواب دادند، "ما به دور
دنیا می گردیم تا شهرهای زیادی را ببینیم." مرد پیر با نگاهی تعجّب آمیز به آن ها
گفت، "مدّت هاست که به خاطر خشک سالی هیچ کس به دیدن این شهر نیامده
است. در این شهر آب آن قدر کمیاب است که هیچ کس خودش را با دیگری
قسمت نمی کند."

گرشاسب و برزوی وارد شهر شدند. همهٔ درخت های شهر خشک و بی برگ بودند.
در هیچ مکان نه گلی دیده می شد نه سبزه ای.

برزو متوجّه شد که چوبدستی تکان می خورد. آن را از کوله پشتیش بیرون آورد و
محکم به دست گرفت. در حالی که راه می رفتند، چوبدستی جادو خود به خود
تکان خورد. و به سویی دیگر اشاره کرد. دو دوست به آن سو روان شدند تا به چاهی
خشک رسیدند.

ناگهان چوب دستی از دست برزوی بیرون پرید و در چاه افتاد. پس از آن به صورتی
جادویی چاه پر از آب شد. مردمی که از آن جا رد می شدند چاه لبریز از آب را دیدند
و از شادی فریاد کشیدند. ماجرای چاه پر از آب خیلی زود به گوش همهٔ مردم شهر
رسید. مردم با دلوها به چاه آمدند، وقبل از همه کودکان و ناتوانان را سیراب کردند.

چندی پس از آن اولّین باران پائیز بارید. باران شهر و مزرعه های خشک اطراف آن را شست، و زمین های خشک را سیراب کرد. آن سال باران هایی فراوان و پر برکت در آن شهر باریدند. در اوّل بهار درخت ها جوانه زدند و دشت ها پر از سبزه و گل های وحشی شدند.

گرشاسب و برزوی زیبایی نورسیدهٔ آن شهر را دیدند و تصمیم گرفتند دست از سفر بردارند و در آن جا ماندگار بشوند. با دو خواهر مهربان و زیبا عروسی کردند، و سالیان سال با خوشی در آن شهر زندگی کردند.

آن شهر یک از زیبا ترین شهرهای دنیا شد، وهر بهار مردمان زیادی به آن جا سفر کردند، تا زیبایی درخت ها وگل های آن را ببینند. چوبدستی جادو همچنان در چاه ماند.

۲۹

دو شاهزادهٔ همزاد

روزی بود روزگاری بود. زیر گنبد کبود پادشاهی بود که دو پسر همزاد و همسان داشت. نگرانی بزرگ پادشاه آن بود که بعد از او کدام یک از آن دو شاهزاده به جای او به تخت شاهی خواهد نشست. پادشاه با عاقلان دربار در این باره مشورت کرد. آن ها پیشنهاد کردند که برای انتخاب ولیعهد بهتر آن است که پادشاه مسابقاتی ترتیب دهد، و گفتند، "شاهزاده ای که در این مسابقات برنده شود، جانشین تاج وتخت معرّفی خواهد شد." دلاوران سپاه پادشاه که در اسب سواری و شمشیر بازی و کمان کشی از همه ماهرتر بودند، مسابقاتی بزرگ را ترتیب دادند.

جشن گشایش مسابقات پر شکوه بود. حیاط بزرگ کاخ با پرچم های رنگارنگ ودرفش های بنفش زر اندود آرایش یافته بودند. شیپورها با نوایی حاکی از پیکار و دلاوری به صدا در آمدند، و پاسداران کاخ با لباس های همشکل و همرنگ شایگان با نوای شیپورها با هماهنگی ازجلو پادشاه و شاهزادگان و بزرگان دیگر گذشتند. پس از تشریفات گشایش، پادشاه شروع برنامه را اعلام کرد.

مسابقات سه روز طول کشیدند. روز اوّل با مسابقهٔ اسب سواری شروع شد. دو برادر با اسب های پرتوانشان با کمال مهارت از روی مانع های بزرگ پریدند، از مسیر های پیچ واپیچ گذشتند، و با سرعتی هرچه بیشتر به خطّ پایان مسابقه نزدیک شدند. هر دو بدون آن که به مانعی برخورد کنند، در یک زمان به خطّ پایان مسابقه رسیدند.

روز دوّم روز مسابقۀ شمشیربازی بود. دو شاهزاده هر یک با شمشیری بزرگ و سهمگین پیکار کرد تا خراشی به لباس دیگری بزند. ولی هیچ یک نتوانست دیگری را بخراشد. ماهرترین شمشیربازان سپاه پادشاه که با دقّت دو برادر را قضاوت می کردند، نتیجۀ مسابقه را برابری اعلام کردند.

روز سوّم روز مسابقۀ کمان کشی بود. کمان کشان ماهر سپاه پادشاه هدف ها را بالا و پایین و در چپ راست گذاشته بودند. هریک باید بود با سرعت اسب سواری کند و همۀ هدف ها را با تیر بزند. دو شاهزاده به یک گونه ماهر بودند و همۀ تیرهایشان درست به مرکز هدف ها نشستند.

در نیمۀ دوّم آن روز، شاهزاده ها باید بود زبردستی خود را در نشانه گیری هدف های دور دست ثابت کنند، هدف هایی آن قدر دور که به سختی می شد آن ها را دید. یک شاهزاده کمان را بالا برد و چندین بار تیر را دقیقاً به مرکز هر یک از هدف ها زد. شاهزادۀ دیگر هم کمانش را کشید و با همان مهارت چندین بار تیر را دقیقاً به مرکز هدف ها زد. ولی، در بار آخر ناگهان دردی شدید در دستش احساس کرد، و دستش را بی اختیار عقب کشید. تیر به هوا رفت، به هدف نرسید و ناپدید شد.

شاهزاده گرچه که از این شکست غمگین شد، ولی سرنوشت خود را قبول کرد. پادشاه یک شاهزاده را به عنوان ولیعهد اعلام کرد، و دیگری را فرماندۀ کلّ سپاه.

چندی بعد پادشاه سالخورده درگذشت، ولیعهد به جای او به تخت شاهی نشست، وبرادر وفادارش فرماندۀ کلّ سپاه او شد.

در سرزمین همسایه خلیفه ای ستمکار سلطنت می کرد، که همیشه با کشورهای همسایه اش سر جنگ داشت، و سعی می کرد کشورهای همسایه را تسخیر کند. آن قدر بی رحم و کژ رفتار بود که همۀ درباریان و خدمتکاران قصر از او وحشت داشتند و همۀ سربازان سپاهش از او متنفّر بودند. او به کم ترین دلیل و گاهی حتّی بدون هیچ دلیلی افراد تحت فرمانش را به زندان می انداخت. یکی از این زندانیان جادوگری عاقل و خوش نهاد بود، که در زندان قصر محبوس بود. جادوگر دو شاهزاده را می شناخت و در گذشته دوست صمیمی پدرشان پادشاه شادروان بود.

خلیفهٔ ستمکار که شنید پادشاه سالخورده سرانجام درگذشته است، با خودش فکر کرد، "پادشاه جوان بی تجربه است. موقعیتی مناسب است که به کشور همسایه حمله کنم و آن جا را تسخیر کنم." فرماندهٔ سپاهش را خواند و به او دستور داد تا تمام سپاه را برای جنگ آماده کند.

خبر لشکرکشی خلیفهٔ ستمکار زود به گوش پادشاه جوان رسید. پادشاه برادرش و وزیران عاقل دربار را خواند تا با آن ها مشورت کند. وزیر دست راست گفت، "چاره ای نیست، باید زود دست به کار شد و سپاه دشمن را شکست داد." وزیر دست چپ گفت "باید آن ها را مجبور به عقب نشینی کنیم تا به خلیفهٔ نگون بختشان بر گردند." برادر پادشاه و فرمانده سپاه گفت، "عقب نشینی دشمن کافی نیست. باید این خلیفهٔ ستمکار را از قصرش بیرون انداخت و مردم آن سرزمین را از شرّ او خلاص کرد."

شبانگاه سپاهیان پرتوان پادشاه جوان به فرماندهی برادر همزادش به راه افتادند. سربازان اسب های خود را با تندی و چالاکی راندند و قبل از طلوع آفتاب با سپاه دشمن روبرو شدند. سپاهیان وحشت زدهٔ دشمن خیلی زود پراکنده شدند، و میلی هم نداشتند که از خلیفهٔ ستم کارشان دفاع کنند.

برادر پادشاه پیشاپیش سپاهش اسب را راند تا به قصر خلیفهٔ ستمکار رسید. پاسداران قصر، که سپاهی چنین پرتوان را دیدند، زود به زانو در آمدند و تسلیم شدند. قصر به دست فرماندهٔ سپاه افتاد. او به سربازانش دستور داد خلیفهٔ ستمکار را پیدا کنند و به زندان بیندازند. وقتی به زندان قصر رسیدند از دیدن آن همه زندانیان از یاد رفته و رنج دیده متحیّر شدند، و خیلی زود همهٔ آن ها را آزاد کردند.

جادوگر چون زندانیان دیگر آزاد شد، و از سربازان درخواست کرد که او را به فرماندهٔ سپاهشان ببرند. وقتی که شاهزاده جادوگر را دید، او را شناخت چون دوست پدر شادروانش بود. جادوگر گفت، "خلیفهٔ ستمکار نمی دانست که جادوی نیک از درون زندان او هم مؤثر است." شاهزاده با تعجّب پرسید، "مقصود چیست؟" جادوگر ادامه داد، "در مسابقات بین شما و برادر عزیزتان، دردی را که در حال کمان کشی

در دستتان احساس کردید تصادفی نبود. از شما طلب بخشش می‌کنم، چون این درد اثر جادوی من بود. مقصود آن بود که شما فرماندهٔ سپاه بشوید، و این سرزمین را از دست این خلیفهٔ ستمکار آزاد کنید.»

شاهزادهٔ فرماندهٔ سپاه پادشاه سرزمینی شد که آن را آزاد کرده بود. دو برادر سالیان سال در دو سرزمین همسایه با صلح و آرامش پادشاهی کردند و به «دو پادشاه عادل» مشهور شدند.

گلیم گوشان و واق واق ها

روزی بود روزگاری بود. زیر گنبد کبود دریانوردی بود که خیلی دلیر بود. به جاهایی در دل دریا رسیده بود که پیش از او هیچ کس کشف نکرده بود، و مخلوقاتی را دیده بود که پیش از او هیچ کس ندیده بود. همراه دریانورد در کشتی ناویاران دلیر و کار آموخته ای بودند که در باد و باران و بوران و طوفان بدون ترس آمادهٔ کمک بودند. همچنین در کشتی جهان دیده ای بود پر از تجربه، که زبان های زیادی را می شناخت، و به هرجا که می رسیدند می توانست با مردم محلّی گفتگو کند.

روزی به جزیره ای رسیدند که پر از مخلوقاتی شگفت انگیز بود. صورت هایشان همچون صورت کودکان معصوم بود. لباس هایشان پر از برگ بود، به رنگ سبزی زیبا، مثل رنگ اوّلین برگهای بهار. و پای هایشان شبیه ریشه های درخت بود. وقتی با هم گفتگو می کردند مثل این بود که سگ ها واق واق می کنند.

مرد جهان دیده به آن ها نزدیک شد و با دقّت به گفتگوی آن ها گوش داد. خیلی زود فهمید که زبانشان زبانی واقعی است و می توانند در بارهٔ همه چیز با هم گفتگو کنند.

دریا نورد به جهان دیده گفت "از آنها بپرس که کی هستند و اسم این جزیره چیست." مخلوقات جزیره داستان زندگیشان را تعریف کردند و گفتند:

"ما قوم واق واق هستیم و نام این جا جزیرهٔ واق واق است. ما نیمی آدم هستیم و نیمی درخت. سالیان سال ما خوش و خرّم در این جزیره زندگی می کردیم. هر سال در اوّلین روز بهار در سینهٔ هر یک از ما و از درون دل ما گلی خوش بو غنچه می زد. وقتی که گل باز می شد ما را شاد می کرد، نیم انسانی ما پر توان تر می شد، و می توانستیم آزاد در این سرزمین رفت و آمد کنیم.

تا که روزی ساحره ای اهریمن صفت از ما خواست تا مثل او بد رفتاری کنیم. چون قبول نکردیم ما را نفرین کرد و با سحر و جادو خاک جزیره را آلوده کرد. چون ما نیمی درختیم، آلودگی خاک گل های دلمان را پژمرده کرد و عمرمان را کوتاه."

دریا نورد به جهان دیده گفت "به واق واق ها بگو اگر بخواهند آن ها را به جنگل گلیم گوشان خواهیم برد." جهان دیده برای واق واق ها از جنگل گلیم گوشان تعریف کرد، و واق واق ها به دقّت به حرف های او گوش دادند:

"جنگل گلیم گوشان در ناحیه ایست دور دست، در راه چین و ماچین. در این جنگل مثل هر جنگل دیگر درخت هایی بزرگ سر به فلک کشیده اند. در شاخه های درختان پرنده های خوش رنگ و خوش آواز لانه دارند، و در بین درختان حیوانات جور واجور رفت و آمد می کنند.

ولی در این جنگل مخلوقاتی دیگر هم هستند که با مخلوقات جنگل های دیگر تفاوت دارند، مخلوقاتی به نام گلیم گوشان. گلیم گوشان مردمانی مهربان و خوش رفتارند که گوش هایی خیلی بزرگ دارند، حتّی بزرگ تر از گوش های فیل. آن ها با مهارت زیاد از درخت ها بالا و پایین می روند و از شاخه ای به شاخهٔ دیگر می پرند.

در عرض روز از درختی به درخت دیگر می پرند تا میوه هایی خوش مزّه پیدا کنند و بخوردند، و در حال پرش گوش های بزرگشان به این طرف و آن طرف می جنبند. شب ها که باد سرد بین شاخه های بزرگ و پر برگ درختان می وزد یک گوششان را روی شاخه ای پهن می کنند و بر آن می خوابند، وگوش دیگرشان را مثل پتو روی خودشان می کشند.

گلیم گوشان نگهبانان جنگلند. و همیشه کوشش می کنند که جنگل سبز و خرّم بماند. آن ها می توانند با آب دهانشان همه چیز را حل کنند. وقتی شاخهٔ درختی خشک می شود، گلیم گوشان دور آن جمع می شوند و آن را می لیسند تا شاخهٔ خشک بیفتد. و بدینسان جنگل همیشه سبز و خرّم و پر از درخت می ماند.

آن ها آشتی گرایند، از جنگ و ستیز بیزارند، و همیشه آمادهٔ کمک به دیگران. از همهٔ مردمی که دیده ام گلیم گوشان از همه خوش رفتار ترند و پاک نهاد تر."

وقتی واق واق ها داستان جنگل گلیم گوشان را شنیدند، راضی شدند سوار کشتی بشوند و به جنگل گلیم گوشان برسند. در راه دریانورد به کمک جهان دیده برای واق واق از سفرهای بی شمارش تعریف کرد. واق واق ها داستان هایی از سرزمین های مختلف و مخلوقات گوناگون شنیدند. از سویی آرزو کردند مانند دریا نورد و جهان دیده دنیا را ببینند، و از سویی آرزویشان آن بود که روزی به جزیرهٔ واق واق برگردند.

سر انجام واق واق ها به جنگل رسیدند. پس از گفتگو با گلیم گوشان، در گوشه ای از جنگل جایگیر شدند. چند ماه گذشت. فصل خزان آمد و رفت. پس از آن باران های زمستان واق واق ها را به حال آورد. عمر واق واق ها مثل دوران قدیم درازتر و دراز تر شد. حالا که بهار فرارسیده بود، باز در سینهٔ هر یک از واق واق ها گلی رویید، وآن گوشهٔ جنگل مکانی شگفت انگیز و پر از عطر شد.

یک شب زیبا در آن بهار ساحرهٔ کژ رفتار از آن جنگل گذر می کرد و گلی زیبا را در سینهٔ یک واق واق خردسال دید. ساحره در یک آن گل را در انگشتان استخوانیش گرفت و آن را از سینهٔ خردسال بی چاره کند. واق واق از درد فریاد کشید، ولی ساحره به تندی از آن جا دور شد. ساحره نیشخندی زد، فریادی از شادی کشید و با خود گفت، "چه چوب دستی جادوی زیبایی را می توان از شاخهٔ این گل درست کرد، و چه پیش آمدهای اهریمنیی را می توان با آن به وجود آورد."

واق واق بی چاره بدون آن گل نمی توانست از جایش تکان بخورد و چون درختی همیشه در یک جا ماند. از آن شب شوم به بعد رفتارش توهین آمیز شد و با همه بد رفتاری کرد. هر چه وقت می گذشت رفتار او بد تر و بد تر می شد. سنگ ها را از

زمین بر می داشت و به دیگران پرتاب می کرد، و بر هر مخلوق معصوم جنگل که از آن جا گذر می کرد نعره و فریاد می کشید.

کم کم آن قدر بد رفتار شد که واق واق های دیگر تاب تحمّل او را نداشتند واز آن گوشهٔ جنگل دور شدند. پرنده های خوش رنگ و خوش آواز دیگر در آن گوشهٔ جنگل پرواز نکردند، و حیوان های دیگر از او دوری جستند. گلهای زیبا هم در آن گوشهٔ جنگل خشک شدند، و واق واق بد رفتار تنها ماند.

گلیم گوشان که نگهبانان جنگل بودند، ویرانی آن مکان را، که روزی بسیار زیبا بود، دیدند وخیلی نگران شدند. بزرگِ گلیم گوشان با خود اندیشید، "به خاطر رفتار بد این واق واق تمام این گوشهٔ جنگل جادویی و زیبا خالی از درخت شده است. ترسم آن است که اگر این ماجرا ادامه پیدا کند، تمام جنگل ناپدید شود." به این خاطر به دیگران گفت برای مشورت در شاخه های یک درخت خیلی بزرگ در میان جنگل جمع شوند.

در این گرد هم آیی، بزرگِ گلیم گوشان از دیگران پرسید، "برای درمان این مشکل چه باید کرد؟". گلیم گوشی جوان گفت، "باید این واق واق بد رفتار را تنبیه کرد." دیگران مخالفت کردند. کم کم جرّ و بحث به داد و فریاد کشید، و برای اوّلین بار بحث گلیم گوشان به دعوا کشید. ساحره که در جایی نزدیک مخفی بود، جرّ و بحث آن ها را شنید و خوشحال شد.

ناگهان همه با شگفتی هما را دیدند که در آسمان پرواز می کند. هما پرنده ای شگفت انگیز بود که همیشه در حال پرواز بود، و به هر جا که می رسید با خود آرامش و شادی می آورد. همه ساکت شدند و دست از دعوا بر داشتند. هما گفت، "ساحرهٔ اهریمن صفت این وضع را به وجود آورده است. هر چه شما خشمگین تر بشوید او قوی تر خواهد شد."

جادوهای ساحره بر هما اثری نداشت. هما به سوی ساحرهٔ کژرفتار پرواز کرد، چوب دستی جادو را از دست او در آورد، به کوه های دور دست آتش زا برد و در آتش انداخت.

یکی از عاقل ترین گلیم گوشان گفت: "اگر نفرت و خشم این گوشهٔ جنگل را خشک کرده است، بیایید تا در دور و بر واق واق بد رفتار درخت بکاریم. در ابتدا که درخت ها کوچکند دست واق واق به آن ها نخواهد رسید. سرانجام، وقتی که ریشه های درختان قوی تر بشوند و شاخه های درختان به او نزدیک تر، حال او به تر خواهد شد." همه گفتند که این بهترین راه است.

گلیم گوشان به گوشه های مختلف جنگل رفتند، ریشه های نهال های کوچک را از زمین رها کردند، و نهال ها را دور واق واق نا آرام کاشتند. درخت ها بزرگ شدند، و شاخه هایشان زود پر از برگ های سبز شدند. گل های تازه در همه جا روییدند، و پرنده های خوش رنگ و خوش آواز به درختان باز گشتند.

شاخه های زیبای درختان به او نزدیک تر شدند. شاخه ای کوچک به سینهٔ رنج دیده و ورم کرده اش نزدیک شد و به نقطه ای رسید که گل زیبایش با بی دادی از او ربوده شده بود. در ابتداء خروشی بر آورد. ولی زود در میان شاخه های سبز درختان احساس آرامشی به او دست داد، وحتّی وقتی نسیم بهار شاخه ها را به بدن درد دیده اش نزدیک کرد به نرمی آهی کشید.

واق واق به یاد روزهای زیبای گذشته افتاد، که دوستانش دور و بر او جمع بودند. کم کم حتّی با آن که گلی زیبا در سینه نداشت، رفتارش را عوض کرد. گلیم گوشان کمک کردند واق واق های دیگر را به آن جا باز گردانند، و او دیگر تنها نبود. در فصل بهار گلی تازه در سینه اش رویید.

بعد از سال ها دریا نورد و جهان دیده به جنگل گلیم گوشان بازگشتند و تغییرات شگفت انگیز جنگل را دیدند. عدّه ای از واق ها سوار کشتی شدند و به جزیرهٔ خود باز گشتند، وعدّه ای در جنگل ماندند. ساحرهٔ پلید ناپدید شد، و همهٔ آن ها سالیان سال با خوشی زندگی کردند.